Shades of Red

Confessions of a Wanna Be Church Girl

Shades of Red

Confessions of a Wanna Be Church Girl

Sapphire

COPYRIGHT

The Butterfly Typeface Publishing
PO BOX 56193
Little Rock Arkansas 72215
www.butterflytypeface.com
butterflytypeface.imw@gmail.com

DEDICATION

For Aaron Elijah

CONFESSIONS

*Have you ever noticed someone who acts like a freak,
talks nasty, etc.?*

It's all there on full display for the world to see.

*I don't care to get to know them. I don't need to,
they've already told me all I need to know.*

*But show me someone quiet, kind, friendly, modestly
acting, and I want to find out what they really do.*

These are my confessions ...

TABLE OF CONTENTS

ACKNOWLEDGMENTS

I thank my family for their unconditional love and my mother for her unyielding faith.

Show me someone quiet, kind, friendly, modest-acting, and I'll want to find out what they *really* do.

FOREWORD

I've only been well for the last few years.

A while back, I'd started going through a lot, a whole lot. I'm pretty strong in my opinions, so when I'm attacked, I'm confronted with a lot of things all at once.

There's not much I care about, so I kind of have to be tried back to back before I'll fold.

I'd worked very hard and bought a home for my baby. I wanted him to have a yard to play in. Things were pretty perfect. I had two vehicles that were paid for. I was making good money finally. Everything was in order. My son's father was living with me again and then just like that, everything wasn't so perfect anymore.

There are no good or bad people. We are all just people fighting daily against our deepest, darkest desires, which are all different. Cursing is as deep as it gets for some, and while others view cursing as nothing, it can be a lot for someone who feels convicted about cursing.

As we move closer to the end of time, it gets harder for people to find a reason why they shouldn't feed their desires that are seemingly part of their very nature. There seems to be a greater pull for us to do wrong. As the end nears, the enemy is desperate to round up his souls. This world is horrible, and sadly it will never get any better. It only gets worse from here.

Over the past few months, I've been thinking a lot about Genesis, Chapter 18:

Abraham asks God, where He is going.

God replied, "I've heard an outcry from Sodom, and if I take a look and find it to be true, I will destroy it."

Abraham asks God how he could destroy the good along with the wicked? He said, "What if there are fifty righteous men who will die among the wicked?"

God says, "If there are fifty righteous men I won't destroy it."

Abraham went all the way down to ten righteous men.

Still, God said, "If I find ten righteous men, I won't do it."

We all know how the story ends. God destroyed the town.

There were not even ten righteous men who remained! He then had to destroy the whole world, saving only Noah and his family. He later promised Noah that He wouldn't flood the earth again but said He would destroy the world by fire.

God created us, and even He does not trust us to do anything more than what is in our nature to do. If left to our own devices, man will turn corrupt every time.

God says, "Put your trust in no man."

I do not, and here on these next few pages, I will attempt to tell you why.

My story isn't a chronological one, but rather a flashback of experiences, memories, and fragmented stories. I share them with you, not for your entertainment, but for you to understand that sometimes there is no explanation for why someone is different.

Sapphire

A WORD FROM THE PUBLISHER

Shades of Red, Confessions of a Wannabe Church Girl is the story of a woman who struggles with a dark desire to control others while balancing being a mom and a believer in Jesus Christ. Her inner conflict threatens her sanity, her ability to parent, and at times even her life!

In the short life of my company, I've been advantaged to read many inspirational stories, stories that have changed my life and encouraged me to 'keep striving for greatness'. When Sapphire's story came to my attention, my initial reaction was one of compassion, curiosity, and if I'm honest, shock.

Were there people who really lived this life? Did black people, women, behave this way? Really?

I struggled not only to find the 'point' in the story, but to believe that the author could actually have actually had these experiences. She didn't 'look' like the 'type.' Which is why it is so important for us to love and accept each other as we are and let God do what God does.

There are passages that are very graphic and explicit. However, there are just as many passages that are spiritual and moving. As I continued to read the manuscript, I relied on my empathetic nature and took a leap of faith that God would direct my steps for the direction of this book. And He did. Midway through the process of publication, tragedy struck and the 'point of it all' appeared in a miraculous way!

This book is different. How the story is presented is different (it is not chronological, nor is it in any particular order – instead we rely on 'flashbacks' and 'confessions' to relay the story.

Shades of Red is just as ambiguous as its author and I challenge you to step away from your preconceived notions and allow yourself to be educated and evolved to a new level of thinking and compassion.

When you're done reading it, ask yourself, "What do you value more than God?"

IN THE BEGINNING ...

The Monster Looks Like Me

"Shut up! Just shut up! You're a weak crybaby. If I see one teardrop, I'm going to hurt you. I mean it, and you know I do."

I stood there, fists tight, breath heavy, teeth clenched, and big crocodile tears begging to be released from my eyes as I stared at my reflection in the mirror.

I'm not sure what I was upset about on that particular day. I couldn't have been but seven years old and in the second grade. More than likely I was upset because my best friend had been bullying me since first grade.

She was very pretty and popular. I was pretty too, but I was regular pretty and as others continued to point out, not skinny. In ballet, we were able to choose to wear bottoms or tops over our leotard if we wanted. I chose to wear bottoms.

I remember that day like it was yesterday.

As I sat in the circle waiting for class to start, I could see her.

Charlotte was a little red-haired, freckled, white girl. Pointing to my chest, she says, "Why do you look like a woman up there?"

I was already getting felt up by the older boys in the hallways. I thought at least in *this* class I wouldn't be harassed. I know she meant no harm, but I got up and switched my bottoms out for a top. So yeah, I wasn't skinny, but I wouldn't say I was fat either.

Anyway, we were both light-skinned and had long hair. Her hair was different. Mine had to be hot combed every Sunday and then put into plaits.

Charlotte would pull my hair and say things like, "Morgan has ten french fries on her head!"

It hurt me, a lot. I don't know why it did. Maybe because I wasn't used to coming up against someone I wasn't sure how to face. Up to that point, I hadn't been afraid of anything or anyone. I quickly realized I didn't like the feeling of fear of any kind, at all.

I believed in God, even at that age.

I even heard Him speak once, just as sure as my name is Morgan Mitchell.

I was on the playground one day with a few friends. We were off closer to the field, away from the others, especially teachers. We were saying bad words. The other kids decided to run off, and I stayed behind just to see what the word 'shit' felt like rolling off my tongue one more time.

"Shit!" I said confidently.

Suddenly out of the clear blue sky I heard, "Stop it!"

I looked around, and it scared the 'shit' out of me. I ran to catch up with my classmates and asked if they'd heard anything. They all said, "no" as we headed back in from recess. I loved God, and I knew He existed for sure, even more so now.

So why doesn't He help me with this girl? I thought.

At church that Sunday, I heard a message that forever changed my life.

"Be careful," the Preacher said. "Satan answers prayers too."

I was much too young to get anything out of the message other than the fact that I could also pray to Satan and he would answer.

So here I stood, in the mirror. In spite of my resistance, a teardrop fell from one of my eyes. I was furious. I began to pinch myself and inhale deeply. As I inhaled deeply, I said, "You are powerful. You don't feel pain."

This then became a ritual of mine anytime I felt weak. I'd punish myself: pinches, pinpricks, burns. I preferred physical to emotional pain. At least that was something I could understand. I was getting tougher, but there had to be another way. I didn't want to feel *anything*.

So, I began to pray.

"Satan," I began. "I love God, but He takes too long. I need your help right now. I have to deal with this girl. Make me strong, make me fearless. Make me strong, make me fearless, make me strong, make me fearless, make me strong, make me fearless."

I said it over and over until I began to laugh and laugh. I laughed hysterically until I felt euphoric. I was literally weak and light-headed. I looked in the mirror, and I looked different. Tears streaked my face, but I no longer felt weak. I felt empty. I felt nothing and feeling nothing felt powerful.

I'm not sure how long it took, but the next time someone decided to bully me, I handled it much better.

We were coming in from recess, and a kid said or did something. I pushed her, and it felt so good, I decided to take it a step further. As we were walking down the steps, I yanked the girl by her pretty little ponytail, and she tripped a step.

Her minions all of a sudden had a heart. "No. Stop; don't do that," they said.

I had to get one more shove in, but the tables had turned.

I'd become the aggressor, and just like that a monster was born, and she looked just like me.

PREFACE
Undiagnosed

I have wondered over the years if I am 'undiagnosed.' The things I think, feel, and do are (as I've come to understand from conversations with my mother) not normal. However, they are normal for me.

I HATE people.

But, I love my son. So much so, that I went on a hiatus from my dual and often unhealthy lifestyle for more than ten years to protect him. That didn't last as long as I would have liked for it too.

Hervey Cleckley's clinical profile, "The Mask of Sanity" written in 1941 and widely used by today's psychological clinicians offers key behavioral characteristics that could point a finger in the right direction to my mental state. In his opinion, I'd likely be diagnosed as a sociopath.

I don't think there is anything wrong with me. Which according to Cleckley, I wouldn't.

I've come to understand that we are most vulnerable during sexual encounters. For me, power and dominance are what I crave, not sexual gratification. I live for the chase and the fulfillment of the kill. I deal with men, but I deal with women too. I'm not gay, or bisexual. As a matter of fact, I don't like pussy at all. That's why I remain fully clothed, and I wear gloves. I don't even want the juices on me.

Do I get off?

Yes, I do, but it's not from sex. It's from the power I take from the people I encounter.

I've been asked if I hate women. No, I don't. I think women are beautiful and I get excited watching them but to eat a pussy or grind on a pussy (well, maybe grinding one with the right chick would be pretty powerful), is something I am not interested in. I will take head from a chick, haven't done it in a while, but it's acceptable if I'm in the mood. Rarely am I. I'm always in the mood for a dude though, well my dude.

So, I guess gender is kind of irrelevant for me in regards to what I do. Power is power.

Some may find it strange (and I do as well) that I don't consider myself gay for the things I do with women, especially since if a dude so much as do anything with another dude, I consider him gay.

Women aren't my only prey. I have stories about making dudes my bitch too. It's harder with them though. You have to make sure you're definitely more dominant. Shit could go left quick, and you'd find yourself in a situation.

I offer this story to you merely as a means of clearing my head because it matters not what you think.

The duality of my life probably makes some people think I'm ashamed or remorseful.

Nothing could be farther from the truth.

I'm very smart. I possess charm. So much so that I know it's a requirement for what I do.

What is it that I do?

Simple. I take control.

AN INITIAL CONFESSION:
I'm Sick, Aren't I?

---

*I don't tell because where's the fun in that. I
like to remain unsuspecting.*

When I met Bruce, I immediately felt like we were
kindred spirits. Not only was he 'fine,' but the way he
understood me and let me be me, was very attractive. He
eventually became my "roommate," and while there have
been plenty of times that I've considered that I'm in love
with him, I know that I'm only drawn to the fact that he
and I are so much alike.

When Bruce and I met we both kind of had a competition
to see who would mess this thing up first because as
different as we were, we were also a lot alike.

He knows I'm "sick." And I think in between meeting me
and now, he has discovered that he's "sick" too.

He HATES people.

Sometimes we argue about who's sicker or a sociopath.

"You need to get help," Bruce insists.

"Why," I ask innocently. "I'm operating at full capacity."

"If *this* is you well and at full capacity, it's pretty bad."

Bruce doesn't know about the secret sex-life stuff. I don't tell most men for different reasons, the ones I actually like that is. I'm convinced they wouldn't be able to handle it.

Not many people know about the *real* me. I keep it under wraps because well if I told people how would I get them to trust me? How could I dominate and control them?

The people in my family know I'm *different* because they grew up watching me do weird stuff. They have come to expect it and to a degree accept it. They're awesome that way, and I thank God for that.

I'm very irresponsible, hardly follow the rules, and would have nothing if it wasn't for my son. I'm a bit spoiled and enabled by my siblings.

My brother is most like me, and we are both more like my dad. My dad's side of the family explains it all away.

We're kind of *normal* for his side of the family. (I've joked with people about it being the inbreeding on that side.)

My mother has become my sounding board. She doesn't understand it really. How could she? She thinks maybe I should try again for diagnosis and treatment.

Full disclosure; I have been treated for depression a few times, but my negativity has nothing to do with my need for power and control. Right now, I'm about 99% emotionally stable, and I *still* do not like or understand people.

Mom knows I have *entertained* women, but not to what extent or why I do it. She knows I *bitch* men and thinks it's sometimes funny and other times gross.

I know she doesn't prefer to hear the things I tell her, but I know that *she* at least will not judge me, keep my secret, and she will pray for me.

Although I tell her a lot, the secret sex-life, I keep to myself. I don't tell because where's the fun in that.

I like to remain *unsuspecting*.

CONFESSION ONE:
My Double Life

"I don't like people very much, never have."

Living a double life gets me access into society.

There is a me that not too many people know about. The person most people see is just generic. It's a reflection of themselves mostly. Whatever energy you give I usually return, depending on the person and the circumstances. Otherwise, I'm just behaving according to what society considers appropriate or "normal."

I'm almost always pleasant or smiling and kind unless I'm distracted, busy or in a hurry.

If I make eye contact with a person, I smile, and I speak. Unfortunately, people mistake this for an invitation. I don't like people much, never have.

Usually, when someone is speaking, I'm thinking inappropriate things.

When I was younger, I thought the things I thought and did were what everyone was thinking and doing.

So, I would often say things like, "they're lying, I can tell," or "they don't really care," or "they were probably thinking they wish I'd hurry up and leave."

My mom said I was cynical, but I told her, "I'm as normal as it gets and if I lie, 99.9% of the time it means almost all people are liars."

That was the first time I was told I was different, but it didn't resonate with me until I was in high school.

I knew most everyone, but most people only knew of me. I wouldn't say I was popular. I got along with most people, and while I didn't lack people to talk to, I really didn't see the point in it.

One day I was speaking with a chick who by society's standards she was more popular than I was. We were talking and laughing and all of a sudden, she asks me about my weekend.

"So, what did you and Meeka get into this weekend?"

"Huh," I was confused. *Why did she think Meeka and I had done anything?*

"What you and your girls do?" She pushed.

"I don't talk to them outside of school," I said matter-of-factly.

The look she gave me let me know that again, I was behaving differently.

The girl she was referring to and a few others were girls I'd hung with through middle school and most of high school. They were my crew, my girls, but for me that only meant that they were just people to help pass the time spent at school. *Why on earth would you want to talk to these people during your free time?*

That's when I realized people like and even enjoy each other's company by *choice*.

That wasn't my experience.

Meeka was probably the only girl in the crew who actually liked me. The others were *my girls* by default. I think Meeka thought we were friends until she realized we weren't.

Someone asked about us once, and in front of Meeka my response to them was, "Oh, we're not friends, we're just cool."

Initially, Meeka thought that was funny, and then it became an ongoing joke for a long time. We'd say it often and even laugh about it. But eventually, it wasn't funny to her anymore.

I apologized to her because I knew that was what I was *supposed* to do. I probably even referred to her as a friend afterward to pacify her.

That was the beginning of me realizing that there are things you *must* do to get people to do what you want them to do.

Most people don't respond well to the truth.

There were two other girls in the neighborhood who were a grade behind me. I did feel closer to them, probably because I'd known them since elementary. One of them lived across the street.

They would try to get me to come out of the house, but I preferred sitting in our dark, damp, creature-infested basement watching scary movies.

I would occasionally imagine that someone or something was behind me, getting closer. I would slowly turn around in hopes that I was about to be a part of a real-life horror movie.

I would invite the girls over to do whatever it was I was doing or catch me later and tell me about whatever it was they found to do. They would spend the night often. Although I'm not sure why; the relationships were pretty abusive. As we got older, they would tell me things I'd done or said to them, and I'd deny it.

Some things I remembered, some I didn't.

I think not remembering was more about me not allowing myself to feel. *If I don't feel it, then it didn't happen. Right?*

I discovered that if I abuse others, then I don't have to deal with being abused. I found a way to release my frustrations, stress, and anger out on others sexually. I found a way to bully someone without feelings of guilt later or the need to "make up." I still hurt people's feelings this way, but it's different in that it seems to be more acceptable.

I really wish I could be one of those people who could just say, "Hey, before you say anything, let me just go ahead and tell you, I don't give a shit."

Living a double life hasn't been a hindrance. I pretty much do as I please. I don't want much so the little I want, I have.

The one thing I don't have is security, but I'm working on marrying someone stable because I feel I will never be secure on my own. I realize I have to have more money in order to be free to be me. You can't really get anywhere in life mistreating people.

I have to pretend so I can get the things I want and need. I'm pretty good at playing the role most of the time, but I do have what I call "glitches."

This is something I watch for in others.

It's hard to be fake *all* the time.

Sometimes you get so frustrated it boils over, and you completely lose it, but then almost as quickly as you lose it, you gather and compose yourself. You apologize, blame it on not eating yet, cry about a dog who died recently or something, and you're back to normal like it never happened.

That's a glitch.

You didn't mean to let the *bitch* slip out.

Normal people don't glitch; there is a slow build up and a slow cooldown period.

CHAPTER ONE: TESTING THE WATERS
Very Well Behaved

We moved into a new neighborhood when I was five years old. My dad just up and bought a house. I didn't know it then, but my mom wasn't involved in the decision process and didn't care too much for the house.

It was a blue split-level home. My mom called on her sisters to help her with the huge job of getting it *decent* and *livable*. It was dirty, outdated, and perfect in my eyes.

While we lived there, I went to three different elementary schools. The first year, I went to kindergarten at a school down the street with my sisters. The next year my sisters were off to middle school, so I was shipped to my paternal grandmother's each morning and afternoon to ride the bus with three of my cousins.

My cousins hated me, which was nothing new to me. I was a favorite grandchild on both sides, so most of my cousins kept their distance. Some of them thought I was a goody two shoes and feared I would tell on them, while others hated me for what I really was, a fake.

We could all be caught doing something, and they would get disciplined while I would get off completely free. I was very well behaved under supervision, very polite, mannerable. Most people saw me as sweet and innocent.

One day, coming home from school, I got beat up by a fifth grader on the bus. My grandmother saw me and immediately spanked all three of my cousins.

"How could yall let Morgan get beat up," Grandma yelled. "How do you sit by and watch your little first-grade cousin get beat up by fifth graders and none of yall help?"

They hollered, "But grandma! Her mouth! She started it!"

I just sat there looking sad and pitiful and innocent. I actually did start the fight and didn't care much that I'd gotten beat up. But watching them get punished for something I'd done, felt good.

Power.

The next year I was at another school.

The two oldest cousins went off to middle school, and I returned to my original school down the street.

Most days it was my job to wake my dad up so he could get me to school. We were late almost all of the time because I simply could not wake him up before my show *Jem* went off.

It was while attending this school, I met a girl who lived down the road from us. She was good with people and knew a lot of the kids in the neighborhood. We would walk home together sometimes. We started to hang out a bit, but that didn't last long. We didn't have a whole lot in common. She was smart and involved in school stuff.

But then one day she asked if I'd go fundraising with her and whatever she won we could split. She really wanted to win first prize, which was a limo ride. I didn't have anything better to do and agreed to go with her. We walked and walked. I just kept her company because I really didn't care about the fundraiser and I didn't think she'd win, and I didn't think she'd take me if she did. Why would she?

One day after fundraising, we were back at my house. I caught her digging in the huge bag of dog food we kept in the kitchen between the fridge and wall. She'd gotten a handful and was just about to put it up to her mouth when I yelled, "What are you doing?!"

She said, "I'm sorry, I wanted to taste the cocoa puffs."

I was overcome with excitement at the thought of what she almost did. I said, "That's not –"

"What? Not what," she asks.

Oh, my wheels were turning. "Nothing. Go ahead, taste it." I could barely contain my eagerness.

She put the dog food in her mouth and made a disgusted face as she crunched.

"Oh my God! You ate dog food," I screamed. "I'm telling everyone at school you eat dog food."

"No, don't ok?" She looked horrified.

I let her off the hook and told her I wouldn't tell. And I didn't. I liked her, something about her kept me from telling. She looked relieved, but I felt powerful knowing that I had something over her that caused her anxiety.

Control.

A few weeks later, she comes over and says, "Guess what?!"

"What?" I asked.

"We won! We're going on the limo ride."

"Really?!" I was excited but kept calm because again why would she *really* take me? No one is just nice like that, right?

Well! The day came, and sure enough, the limo took us and like four other kids to Burger King and around town before dropping us back off at home.

She smiled and smiled the whole ride. I enjoyed it, but I enjoyed watching her enjoy it more. It looked as if she was experiencing it in a way that I wasn't.

We kept in touch, but again we were so different there really wasn't anything to build a *real* friendship on.

One day she came over, and she was looking at things in my room. She would ask about different things, and I would tell her what it was and what it did. Some things I lied about causing her to say, "Really?!" and "Wow!"

Then she picked up my Frisbee and said, "Do you ever play with this?"

I took it from her and said, "Yeah, all the time."

Something came over me and I pushed her on the bed and put the frisbee in between her legs.

"This is what it's for!"

She was half screaming my sister's name and half laughing. What started as what I'd consider innocent playing, soon turned into a struggle. She was fighting with all her might to keep her knees together while trying to get up from my bed all at the same time. I just kept pushing and pushing. It must've hurt towards the end. It had to. I was pushing and sawing back and forth like I was trying to saw her up the middle.

My parents worked a lot, so my sisters and I were at home alone a lot.

I heard my sister yelling from another room, "Morgan! What are you doing?!" She yelled not bothering to get up. "I'm telling Mama and Daddy if you don't stop bothering her."

I kept going until it sounded as if my sister might get up.

"Ok, ok you can get up." I said, but not wanting to stop.

She was blushing as she didn't know what to think. "Why'd you do that?"

I gave her some reassuring pats and said, "I was just playing." And then to normalize things I added, "Can we hang out tomorrow?"

She shook her head, yes, and I walked her out.

I never messed with her like that again. She was a nice girl. We would still see each other now and again until she ended up moving away to another state and then I never saw her again.

That is until she contacted me a few years ago on Facebook.

It was a simple message:

"Hey, how are you?"

I stared at the message, reminiscent for a moment. *Wow, why would she reach out? Does she remember what I did?*

My reply was simple.

"Hi, I'm well and glad to see you are. I've thought about you often over the years. How are things?"

I checked every day for a reply.

Nothing.

Until one day her account disappeared altogether.

CONFESSION TWO:
Glitches and Lies

"I was very cynical growing up."

My mom was 17 and carrying a set of twins when she found Jesus. A few years later she and my dad married. They decided they wanted a boy to complete their family having had two girls already.

I ruined that plan.

Being a bald baby made it easier for my dad to tell people I was a boy anyway. He called me "Junya" (country for junior).

Dad was always telling me how coming up I wasn't scared of much. He said, "When you came into the world you didn't even cry. You opened your eyes and started looking everybody in their faces. After looking at every person in the face *then* you cried."

I took that as a sign that I've always been able to read people and their true intent.

My mom had us in church every Sunday, most Sunday nights, Wednesday nights, Friday nights, and practices on Saturdays. She didn't wear makeup, and her skirts and slips kissed her ankles. She didn't wear pants or shorts. We grew up listening to mostly gospel. Our parents didn't curse, and we hardly ever heard them argue.

Somewhere along the way, my dad started showing what I call *glitches*. Glitches are when you can no longer hide who you really are. The real you begins to slip out.

He wasn't going to church as much anymore either. If we rode with him, we got to hear what was *foreign* to us, a station playing worldly music.

Sometimes instead of going to church with my mom, we'd stay at home with my dad. I would often watch horror movies with him. We were tight at one point, but time together became less and less frequent starting around 3rd grade.

The older I got, the more I understood him.

One day he'd be one way and the next he could be someone completely different. More and more, I felt like

I was more like him than not. There was a war going on inside of me, and I couldn't decide which team I wanted to be on.

Dad tried his best to talk to us and prepare us for the world. We just didn't understand, and he didn't go in depth. He wanted us to know, but he didn't want to scare us I suppose. One of the things he talked about was niggas.

I was in middle school when he said, "Stay away from niggas."

I thought I'd shock him and said, "Well hey, what do you want me to do, be a lesbian?"

It turns out he shocked me because his response was, "If you think you could, yeah, that'd be your best bet."

My dad hated men. He was sure to let us know it.

I think my dad knew how *sick* men could be. I think on some level my dad was *sick*. I wish he'd spoken to me more about it.

I think I'm *sick* too.

It's taken me a long time to come to this conclusion as I've always thought I'm as normal as normal gets.

If I do *it* everyone does *it*.

It being whatever I do.

Which is why I never trust anyone.

I knew lying was something I enjoyed, yet initially I thought of it as playing jokes.

My mom put an end to that notion by saying, "If you don't let the other person in on the joke, it's lying."

So, is there a difference between glitches and lies? In both instances, there is the element of dishonesty.

Glitches make you weak because it exposes the cracks in your armor.

I'm not sure which offers you more power and control, but I think the more lies you tell, the more likely you are to glitch.

CHAPTER TWO: JUST CALL ME RED
I'm Not The Problem

One day I was home, and my sister told me someone was at the door. I go to the door, and there's Steven standing on our porch. He was with his friend Eric. I was only twelve, but something about being pursued won me over instantly.

Steven was tall, had hazel eyes, baby smooth skin and full lips that sent *my lady* into spasms. He also went to our church. *How perfect was that, right?*

My mom asked my dad's permission for us to talk on the phone. The rule was not until you're sixteen, but Dad approved since the boy was *a good church boy* and his parents were preachers.

We became inseparable

Steven wanted to wait, but before I could turn thirteen, I'd convinced him I *wanted* to lose my virginity. As far as I knew we were basically married, so I was ready. He wasn't a virgin and even at age fourteen, he wasn't small at all. So, it took some easing and working and changing positions before we were successful.

Over the next few years we went through a lot.

He'd given me a ring. I called it an engagement ring, but all of the adults called it a promise ring. It was ¼ carat cluster. I discovered there were actually only five tiny diamonds and the rest of the ring was silver to make it all look like diamonds. It didn't matter, we knew we were getting married, so we knew what it was.

I was a bit of a wild child. I would push Steven to his limits, and looking back on it, he was really sweet about it.

At the time, I remember telling my mom there was something a bit feminine about him. I couldn't explain it, and she couldn't imagine it, but there was just *something* about him that made me run from him. Then I'd work really hard to get him back.

My mother and I were convinced the problem was me. She would say, "You have ruined that boy."

Steven and I were on again, off again for years.

During 11th grade I had my mom transfer me to another high school. The moms of the group of girls I'd been hanging with all felt I was a bad influence on the group. It wasn't the first, second or even third time parents had expressed that they didn't want their kids hanging around me.

I didn't feel like I was the problem, so I decided to leave for my own good, start over, focus on school and my future. I knew a few kids at this new school, including Steven's best friend, Eric.

Eric wasn't as 'pretty' as Steven, but he was handsome and definitely had more swag. He was tall, athletic and commanded attention just by entering a room. He had power. He was also the ex-boyfriend of a girl I hung out with, Alexus.

One day, I saw Eric standing at the end of the hall. He was a cutie, and very popular. He was actually way smoother and had way more *street cred* than Steven. That day for some reason something spoke to me and said, *Steven is going to do something to you one day. Get him for it now.*

I was cute that day. This was during one of the phases where I'd wear dresses and heels and really play up the 'girly' thing.

Eric was standing there talking to all of his boys. He glanced at me, threw a hand up and asked, "What's up Red?"

Steven's friends at the other school had given me that name a few years back, and it just stuck.

I walked right up to him and pressed my body into his. I leaned in and whispered into his ear, "When you done, let me hit that," and I walked off.

I heard him whisper first, "Red. Red!" Then he hollered because I'd kept walking, "Red!"

I finally turned around, "Yes?"

"When?" He asked.

"You tell me."

He smiled and said, "Alright."

Not too long after that, we met up. He'd arranged for us to go to a mutual church family member's house in his neighborhood.

It didn't last long, there was no emotion shared, but we both got what we came for. We hooked up a few more times. One of which was on a night Alexus was hanging out with me. I excused myself from the group to meet my friend's ex-boyfriend.

Me, Alexus, and a group of other girls had gone downtown for a social event, and Eric was downtown on business. Eric was scholastic, and his parents were prominent figures in the community. They kept him involved in leadership programs and what not.

We met up in the room he had for the night. I remember him kissing my body and going low.

I said, "No, no," and pulled his head up.

I didn't know what he was doing, and I didn't want to find out. I'd never had anyone's head that close to *my girl* before and it just didn't seem right.

He said, "I'm not, I'm not."

He lingered a while longer but decided to come back up as he knew I wasn't comfortable. Afterward, I returned to the group as if nothing happened.

I thought of Eric as someone special to me. I felt like I could count on him for anything.

I remember one of his goons, who I'd known from elementary, was bothering me one day, harassing me about having sex. I went to Eric and told him about it. The next day in class his goon got down on his knees and apologized as he kissed my hand asking me to forgive him. Eric never had to get his hands dirty. His goons wouldn't let anybody touch him.

He had power and I loved it.

One day I called him because I'd run away. I'd decided to move in with my cousin Tonya who was becoming more like a sister. Tonya was eight years older than me and had three children.

I would watch her kids a lot. Sometimes she'd leave me weed as part of my payment. I never smoked while watching her kids. I took watching her kids very seriously.

Anyway, I decided I was old enough to live with Tonya.

"Mom, I've decided I'm not coming home," I said. "I'm going to live with Tonya; she says it's ok."

"Ok," Mom said nicely and calmly.

"I will still go to school and get a job and help her around the house," I offered.

Again, my mom said, "Ok."

"Ok, I will talk to you soon," and just as I'm about to hang up the phone I hear her say …

"Oh yeah, by the way, your dad and I will be coming by shortly to pick up your car."

"Fuck!" I said, but it sounded more like, "OK," after it came out of my mouth. We hung up the phone.

I told Tonya my mom said, "Ok."

"Oh, cool, cool." That was something she liked to say.

I walked around the house and looked in my new room. It didn't look as appealing as my room at home, especially now that I wasn't going to have a car. I sat in the living room and watched TV as I pretended to be happy and free. I heard noise outside and peeked through the window; I watched my parents repo my car. I tried to keep the lump from swelling up in my throat.

Moments later I called Eric.

"Hey, I have to tell you something," I said.

"Ok."

"I ran away," I blurted.

"Come on Red, you know that wasn't smart. That's no good."

We talked for a few minutes, but it didn't take long before I said, "Can you pick me up and take me home?"

"I'm on the way."

I called my mom and told her I decided to come home. My punk ass couldn't make it an entire night.

"Ok," she said and hung up the phone.

I'm thinking damn, on tv the white moms cry and say, "Becky we will work things out so we're all happy and I'm so glad you decided to come home. I love you." I was thinking, my mom really doesn't care one way or the other. I knew I needed my car, so whatever.

Eric arrived, and I hopped in his car. We have a good 20 minutes to talk. One of the things he mentions is to never sleep with any of his boys from the North Set. He said, "It sounds horrible, but while you're with one, the other eight are in the closet waiting to run a train on you. Don't trust any of them."

It didn't surprise me. He actually lived behind North Set in the big houses. But he ran with the North Set crew, who were well-known guys. That's where his *street cred* came from, rolling with them.

I returned to my high school for my senior year. None of the things we did had stopped us girls from getting into trouble. My girls would often page me and would even come to the school sometimes to check me out due to "emergencies." I told you, it wasn't *me* who influenced them.

Tonya eventually moved into my neighborhood, and we became even closer. Sometimes she would drink until she would begin to cry and tell me details of her rough childhood. I would just hold her and listen. It was really way too much for me to take at such a young age. But I had to be strong for her. I became very overprotective of her and tried to be there for her as much as possible.

Then I moved away to a nearby town to help out one of my sisters who was now pregnant. Guess who was going to school in that town?

Eric.

Of course, we hooked back up. One night he went on to tell me how he'd always had feelings for me going back to first grade. (I forgot to mention, that's when we first met.) He also went to our church when he was younger. He said, "That's why I used to be so mean to you. I was jealous of you and Steven."

He did try to come between Steven and I a lot.

I took it all in and smiled, but in my mind, I smelled bullshit. It could be true, but I had my doubts.

One night after we were done having sex, as we lay there together talking, Eric says, "I think we should end this. I think we're getting too close and our families are too close. If we get close and don't actually get married, I think they'd be hurt. Or what if we have a baby and ruin all of this?"

"Ok," I replied.

Again, I felt it was bullshit, but what can you say other than, "ok."

We remained cool.

I wasn't hurt and in the back of my mind, I couldn't help but be reminded of how right I'd been about caring for someone. This just confirmed how bad of an idea it is.

When you love someone, they have power over you.

CONFESSION THREE:

Intentions Matter

"Everything had to be on my terms."

Sandy and Alexus lived on my street. We all went to school together and rode the same bus. They were both a grade behind me. We soon became a little group and were almost inseparable. They would spend the night with me often on the weekends. Where ever I went, a lot of the times at least one of them would be with me. I didn't go to their homes much.

Everything had to be on my terms for the most part. I had to be in control. Every now and then my mom would catch wind of a conversation, and she'd interject.

"Hey! Don't treat your friends like that," Mom said. "I don't know how you girls even call Morgan your friend. I wouldn't be friends with someone who treated me that way. Morgan if I were your age I wouldn't be friends with you."

I thought my mom was a traitor. *Why wasn't she on my side?*

The girls didn't listen to my mom and would try to get me out of the house often, but I preferred sitting in the dark, alone, watching scary movies.

I even acted out a scene once.

My baby brother had come along by the time I was eight. One night, I crept into his room. I moved very slowly and quietly just like in the movies. I picked up a pillow and lifted it high above my head. I continued moving slowly toward his crib. I began to lower the pillow down into the crib towards his face. Right before getting there my mom says, "What are you doing?"

"I was going to put the pillow under his head," I replied.

She looked puzzled. I'm not sure how long she watched me before saying, "Why were you holding it that way then?"

She asked about it several times over the years. I eventually told her I was acting out a scary movie.

Honestly. That's really what I remember my intentions being.

Anyway, even with my friends insisting we go out, I wouldn't budge. I would tell them to either come in and do what I'm doing, or they could catch me later and tell me about what happened.

The relationships were pretty abusive emotionally. I didn't bother them much physically. I cared about them, way more than I had anyone else who wasn't family. I'm sure they felt I had a funny way of showing it.

Sandy, who lived across the street, was just a pure, innocent sweetheart and it annoyed me quite a bit. I would sneeze, and she'd say, "Bless you."

I'd fall, and she'd ask, "Are you ok?"

I hated that!

I remember one time in particular when I snapped after she called to check on me when I was sick. "Don't ever ask me if I'm ok again," I yelled at her. "Of course, I'm ok; I don't need you checking on me like that!"

"Ok, I'm sorry," she said.

"And stop saying you're sorry," I yelled. "Just stop being so nice!"

Not knowing what else to do she'd just say, "Ok."

I remember talking with my mom about it one day and telling her how weird Sandy was, and how I didn't understand why she would do such a thing. My mom explained that when people care about you, they check on you and show concern.

Well, I didn't like it. It was just annoying.

In spite of me and my rants, we actually managed to have a lot of fun together over the years. As we got older, they would tell me things I'd done or said to them, and I'd deny it. Some things I remembered, some I didn't.

Sandy told me about the time she showed me a pretty little trinket.

"I like it," I said. "It's mine now." I took it from her.

"No," she cried. "You can't have it, my aunt who passed away gave it to me."

"Well thank your dead aunt for me," I said callously; the need for power present even then.

When she told me about this, I denied it to her, but I did remember. I think I gave it back at the end of the day.

Alexus told me about the very first day we met.

I was in fourth grade, and she was in the third. I told her about a fifth grader, Lorenzo and his fourth-grade brother Byron at school who I thought was cute.

"If I don't see Lorenzo today, I'm going to punch you," I said.

The boys rode our bus, so I can't imagine why we wouldn't see him. Anyway, she says she remembered thinking, "Please let us see Lorenzo."

We didn't, and I punched her hard in the arm.

This I don't recall.

She says she should have ended things right then before it even got started.

However, I do remember another girl on the bus who liked Byron, and he was paying her a little too much attention. So, on the playground one day I came across a frog. I saved the frog until the end of the school day. I sat behind her on the bus and slipped it into her lunchbox when she wasn't looking.

"Veronica," I sang and smiled. She already knew I didn't like her because I would frequently yank on her ponytails on the bus rides. She looked at me suspiciously. I'm sure, wondering what I could possibly want. "Look in your lunch box," I continued sweetly.

"Why?" She asked cautiously.

"It's a surprise in there," I responded.

Veronica opened the lunch box and screamed her head off while slamming it shut. Not before the frog could stick a leg out in an attempt to escape. After slamming it shut that leg fell right into her lap, and that just sent her over the top.

Byron felt sorry for her, and it actually made them closer.

Who cares, I thought. *There's still his brother Lorenzo.*

There used to be a time when I blamed my behavior on middle child syndrome; just a neglected kid who needed attention, whether it's good or bad.

Now that I'm older, I am still referred to as weird, mean, annoying, crazy, psycho, and all kinds of other things. I've also been called competitive. When faced with it, I feel its my job to aniliate it.

I'm starting to believe that a tiny bit of what *they* say is true.

CHAPTER THREE: ONE-SIDED THINKING
I Snapped

I moved in with my sister, who was pregnant at the time, but after about a year and a few months, she informed me that she'd be moving out and that I wasn't coming with her.

Trying to make it on my own didn't work, so I returned home. Eventually, I got my own apartment and asked Alexus, my childhood friend, to be my roommate. Then one of my male cousins asked to move in with us. He's gay. Alexus was reluctant but what could she say? I was in control.

It wasn't long before Alexus missed a payment. She, my cousin and I were sitting in my room, on my bed discussing her finances when things got really bad, really quick.

"Now explain to me one more time why you can't make the rent," I asked sarcastically.

"Morgan, I'm sorry," Alexus said scrambling for an answer to appease me. "I have other obligations I need to meet."

That *really* wasn't an answer in my opinion, and I just wasn't able to understand what she meant by that. I was boiling. I looked over at my cousin who was making an 'I don't know what to tell you' face, complete with raised eyebrows. Then I looked back at Alexus, and she was looking just as lost.

I snapped.

I stood up and pushed her face into the pillow on my bed. She was struggling to get up. A part of me wanted to stop. It was a very small part though. The bigger part of me was saying, "Hold her just a little longer; hold her until she stops moving."

I looked over to my cousin, who was *trying* to look unbothered, but he was shifting his body which was a clear signal that he was more than a bit concerned.

I continued to hold her head firmly into the pillow for what seemed like forever. I wanted to kill her, badly.

But I let go.

One of the problems a person like me has sometimes is thinking one-sided. The consequences of attempting to kill Alexus were never considered until they became my reality.

What do *you* think *you* would do if someone tried to smother *you* and then let you go?

I hadn't thought that far in advance.

As soon as I let her go, she pounced on me. She didn't land a hit before I could grab her by the back of her head. She was lying on top of me throwing punches. I was holding her by the hair with my left and blocking her blows with my right, so she still hadn't hit me.

This goes on for a while until my cousin grows tired of waiting for a *real* fight. He picks Alexus up and throws her across the room. I shoot him a look of disapproval.

"What?" He says. "I'm not about to watch *that* all night."

Alexus left out crying and called the police.

While we waited for the police to arrive, we hid a few of her things we wanted to keep for ourselves. The cops showed up and allowed her to get what she could find. She told the cops there was more, but they wouldn't do anything about it. She left still sobbing. My cousin left soon after.

Later, I was chilling in my room, not thinking past *the moment*.

Until *the moment* came knocking on my door.

Alexus' aunt, male cousin and some other family member were banging on my door. I headed towards the door to secure it because they were banging HARD. The male cousin kicks the door open, almost too easily. I turn to head for my room.

He says, "Don't run now."

"I'm not running," I say over my shoulder. "I've got something for you."

I return with a hammer-mallet-type thing.

He says, "I want your cousin anyway."

"Well, he's not here," I explained.

"Alexus told us that ya'll jumped her and I don't think it's right for a dude to be fighting on a girl."

"I never saw him hit her," I said. "and the beef was between her and me."

The aunt has a few things to say and I calmly, as if I'm doing her a favor, let her in on some information I had about her.

"You know," I began all too happy to wipe that smug grin off her face. "I don't know why you're here acting like you care anyway. She says you don't care about her at all. You know what else she says. She says the only reason you raised her was to get the extra money from your mom. But instead of using it to help with her expenses you kept it for yourself. She also said part of the reason she can't pay me rent is because you stole her insurance money her grandma sent to pay her bills. I don't believe you would do her like that, would you? So do you honestly believe I've done her as wrong as she told you? Who do you believe? Who should I believe?"

You could tell by her expression that she was thinking about the things she had done, and the things Alexus had obviously said because how else how would I know any of that.

She became uncomfortable, and they all left.

When you have power, you have to be careful not to get too cocky.

Thinking ahead is always a requirement.

CONFESSION FOUR:
A Normal Church Girl

"There are kids like me out there ..."

In my childhood diary, I wrote that I had been raped. My mom discovered my 'confession,' and she and my dad asked about it. I told them I'd made it up and that it was something I'd heard about.

The truth was, it was my way of taking ownership for something horrible that I'd participated in.

I remember it like it was yesterday and I know it won't be something I'll easily forget.

I attended summer camp twice in my youth. I believe once was when I was around seven or eight and the other time I was around ten or eleven.

While I cannot remember exactly the age, I vividly remember the girl's name, what she looked like and exactly what she was wearing down to her light-colored romper.

This is a memory I'd buried deep and hadn't told anyone, until now.

Sidney was really skinny and had a dark complexion. She needed someone to look after her, and I made it my business to be that person. Well, that was my intention anyway. We were sitting in something much like a lifeguard stand. It was rectangular and had two levels, almost an incomplete tree house.

I'm sure the *Department of Parks and Rec* used it for something. She and I were using it to have "girl talk" I suppose. We were away from the playground where the counselors and kids were.

A boy comes over to join us.

He touched Sidney inappropriately and she giggled and swatted his hand. Then he reached over to me. I swatted him too, but I didn't giggle or find it funny.

By this time, I'd gotten to where I didn't enjoy being touched, but I very much liked being in control.

The boy reached back over to Sidney, and this time I joined in. *Better her than me*, I thought.

I held whatever parts of her frail body that I could while he did whatever it was he wanted.

Her giggles quickly turned into "Stops" and "Nos." I remember her clothes becoming disheveled as parts of her body became exposed. I can't remember how or why it ended. But when it did, she was in tears. He left, and I stayed behind and helped her compose herself.

"Are you ok," I asked as I helped fix her clothes and wipe her tears.

She didn't tell and neither did I or the boy. The camp ended, and I never saw her again.

Writing about it in my diary and claiming it was me was my way of saying what I should have said to her, "I'm sorry."

Every now and then the memory haunts me.

It is just *one* of the reasons I'm a big advocate for keeping your *own* two eyes on your kid as much as possible.

There are kids like me out there, and I considered myself just a normal, good, church girl.

I really wish the story had gone more like, "We both kicked his butt."

Now that I think back, I was more concerned with how powerful it felt to control someone else than I was with how Sidney felt over being powerless.

CHAPTER FOUR: HEARING FROM GOD
Obedience

There are moments when my past revisits me or God Himself will speak to me, and I begin to seriously wonder what's real and what isn't.

For instance, once I was awakened out of my sleep by a voice that said, "Pray for your husband."

I'm not married, I thought. The only person I could think of was Steven.

"Lord, I don't know if you're talking about Steven and what I should pray for, but please let him be ok and touch him at his point of need," I prayed.

It is always good to be obedient.

After me, Steven began dating another girl from our church, and it got pretty serious.

One day at a visiting church, I saw him sitting with her. Looking at her, I could see that she was pregnant. As I walked past them, he reached out to me, and I pulled away.

Later I found out they weren't even together yet and the baby wasn't his. He was trying to talk to me that night, but I was playing hard to get. I liked being chased. It was powerful.

Anyway, after that, he contacted me and asked if I wanted to hang out with a group from the church after service and for me to invite whoever else I wanted. So, I did. Later that night he was driving me home, and before I got out the car, he says, "Tell me what you know."

"What do you mean?" I asked.

"Tell me what you know, because I had a dream, that I was walking down the aisle to you and you had on all white."

"Oh My God. Oh My God. Oh My God," I say stunned. "I have to go; I have to get out of here." I jumped out of the car and ran into the house.

He didn't pull off, so I went back outside and got back in the car.

"This is just so freaky because God woke me up a couple of weeks ago and asked me to pray for my husband," I confessed.

"So, what do you think about that?" He asks.

"I'm not ready to get married," I said. "I actually thought I was called into the single ministry to serve God like Paul."

He laughed. "Well it looks like God called you to be with me."

I guess my confession about the dream I had, helped him decide what to do. He took my dad to lunch and asked his permission and had written my mom a note too.

"Marry me," he said pulling out my old ring. He had even had it polished. "But we have to keep it on the hush for now. Demetia is crazy, and she's threatened to hurt herself and her other two kids if I leave her."

"Umm ok," I said, "but you need to fix that."

I tried to honor his request, but one night he says, "I know your mom is friends with Demetia's mom and aunt, but you should tell her to stay away from them. The family is crazy, and they've started lies that I'm gay."

"What!" I shout as old feelings began to resurface. "Are you?"

"How could you even ask me that Red? You know me."

I noticed he didn't answer the question and then I immediately told my mom what he said and reminded her of what I'd said to her about him being *feminine*.

Over the next few weeks, things were just weird, and I did what I do best when I can't control the situation.

I ran, I broke it off.

Then I did what I do second best, doubted myself and tried to get him back.

We never officially got back together.

However, he told me to continue making wedding plans. I was going to, but my mom said she didn't think that was a good idea.

One night we were in my car on the way to buy shampoo, so I could wash his hair at his parents' house. I kept looking in the rearview mirror. There was a car following us. I didn't recognize the car, but the face looked familiar.

"Is there anything you want to tell me before I embarrass us all?" I asked already feeling irritated.

"No, what do you mean?"

"Someone is following us; do you know who it is?"

"No," he says.

Ok, I thought. *So, we're all getting embarrassed today.*

I drive to my aunt's house where all of my family is gathered for a yard sale. I hop out my car, go to the driver's side window of the car that followed us and sure enough, it's Demetia.

"If you want him, take him. But if you ever drive up on my car that close again I'm going to handle you," I said, realizing I meant every word.

My cousin Tonya immediately runs over and gets into Steven's face and yells, "And you! You need to make up your mind WHO you gonna be with."

My girl had my back.

Steven got into the car with Demetia and left.

I'm not sure where they went, but later he said I could meet him at his house to discuss things. I go over, and before I could enter the house, Demetia pulls up. I immediately knew I was going to draw this out knowing she'd be waiting outside. All I kept hearing her say was, "You better tell her before I tell her."

We went in and began pretty much finalizing things.

I cried, hollered, and yelled out unnecessary questions. His mom was there, and I wanted to know if she knew all of this was going on.

Her answer, "Not to this extent," only made me cry and holler even more.

Finally, I was out of things to make up to do, so it was time to leave. I walked out, looked over at Demetia, smiled and waved.

You see, ever since I was little and had developed that routine for training myself how to cry, it was hard for me to cry for real.

I can cry on demand, but if I'm hurt, like really hurt it's next to impossible for me to shed a tear.

Instead, I get a really bad piercing headache, because even though I may *want* to cry, I've trained myself to hold it in. I have to say, holding it in hurts in way more ways than one.

It feels powerful to be in control of your own tears.

Needless to say, I'm great for crying scenes at church. I can command real tears, hollering and screaming, the whole sanctified works!

It turns out Demetia *was* pregnant with Steven's baby.

Steven and I remained friends. I would still visit him at his apartment sometimes. I was having a really hard time trying to wrap my head around what had happened.

I thought for sure we heard God.

CONFESSION FIVE:

The Holy Ghost

"God, if you don't give me the Holy Ghost I'm not going to make it..."

Things began to happen to me, spiritual things. I was seeing things, suspicious of people, and hearing things. I was legitimately worried that someone was out to get me to the point where I was having panic attacks and felt that there was a *dark figure* after me.

I remember one time I'd gotten so scared that I felt I'd be dead by the age of 21. I typed out a letter for my mom in case I was found dead.

The year I turned 21 was horrific for me.

Three months before my birthday, I was in such turmoil that I asked one of my friends, Matt, for a gun. I think he wanted $300 for it. I don't remember if I actually paid him for it or not. I'd run up a hefty bill with him in other areas as well and I know I never paid that.

It was a cute little revolver.

Matt pushed back his matted dreads and got in my face, "If you ever kill anybody, leave the gun there. Make sure you handle it with gloves at all times. That way when you leave it, they can't trace it back to you without fingerprints," he instructed. "This gun has bodies on it," he said matter-of-factly. "So, make sure you don't keep it if you kill somebody. If they find it on you, you can be charged for the other murders as well. Also, never, never tell them I gave it to you. Then I could possibly be charged with those murders."

"Ok," I replied.

I'd only signed a six months lease where I was living at the time, and my parents wanted me to come home. I told them I would once the lease was up. Meanwhile, I began to feel different. Sometimes I would sing songs that just came from my heart out to the Lord and my teeth would begin to chatter. It just felt weird. I started going back to church, and it was Holy Ghost year and convocation was coming up. I started to feel like the things going on was God trying to reach me before I died.

"Mom, I think I'm about to get the Holy Ghost."

"Oh, ok." She said.

I don't think she believed me. I was so far from saved. I hadn't even been going to church until recently. I kept going. I was trying in church, and I was trying at home too. I found myself *desperate* for Jesus. I would go in my bathroom, in the dark, and to cry out to the Lord.

"God, if you don't give me the Holy Ghost I'm not going to make it," I cried. "Save me, sanctify me and fill me with the Holy Ghost."

Suddenly, the room began to show signs of brightness, like pulsating light coming in dimly and then fading back out. I began to utter, "Nah nah nah nah nah nah nah." The sounds were just leaving my mouth so fast. I knew what *it* was, and I got so excited.

I said, "God I thank you for the Holy Ghost, but if I'm going to make it, I need something stronger. I need more Lord. Give me more."

Then the whole room became illuminated, and a bright white figure swooped in from the ceiling, around the room and entered my back. I began to speak whole words in an unknown tongue.

I was in the bathroom for I don't know how long, but it seemed like forever, and I never wanted it to end. When I finally came out, I saw everything differently. The dark figure was no longer chasing me. I realized that maybe what I'd been anticipating was a *spiritual* death, but the enemy was trying to trick me into believing it was a *physical* death that was coming just to try and drive me crazy.

I remember calling my mom and telling her; *I got it.* She was happy. I moved back home and was truly a new person.

One day my mom was in her bathroom primping. My dad and I were in their room just chit chatting. He picked up one of his guns and started talking to me about it. My mom started squealing from the bathroom as she was not comfortable with the situation at all. My dad was doing his best to quiet her down. But then what I said next only served to make things worse for her.

I say, "I have a gun."

My dad looks over at me and says, "You do not."

"Yeah I do, it's in the car," I replied. I always rode with it under my seat.

"Go get it," he says.

"Ok," I reply and excitedly run out to the car. I bring the gun back in and hand it over to my dad.

He opens it and says, "This gun is fully loaded!"

My mom starts screaming again.

After looking it over, "Sell it to me," Dad says. "You're saved now and anyway the way you drive it's unsafe for you to have it."

I'm hesitating.

"I tell you what, you can sell it to me for $150, or I will trade you for one of mine."

He's right, I thought, *I'm saved, and I've got Jesus to protect me. There is no need for an illegal gun.* So, I sell him my gun.

Here's the part that most people would miss about this story.

What did my dad know that would have him want to get *that* particular gun off my hands?

He wasn't against me *having* a gun, he just didn't want me to have *that* gun. He was even willing to trade me for one of his. Maybe he noticed the missing serial number and was really trying to protect me or perhaps he wanted his own *throwaway* gun.

Which now that I think about it, how would he even know all that if he didn't have some sort of *creep life* history!

Power recognizes power.

CHAPTER FIVE: RESISTANCE & CONTROL
Ménage à trois

I was starting to stray a bit when my aunt Becca and cousin Tonya asked me to hang out with them at this club downtown called *Trois*. They told me to ask about VIP. That's when I saw Deondre. He was a massive man, well over six feet, caramel colored skin and a shiny bald head. I walked over to him and asked about VIP. He told me the details and then asked me to step out back with him.

"Why?" I asked.

"I just want to give you my number."

I stepped out back, and he spoke to me real smooth like. We talked briefly and exchanged numbers and went back in. Aunt Becca, me and Tonya set up our VIP and danced within our own space getting drunk the rest of the night.

I was trying hard to stay on track. I wanted to remain saved.

I also wanted Deondre. I fought the temptation.

Deondre started courting me, but he wanted sex. I hadn't had sex in about two years, as I considered myself very much saved. When I wouldn't put out, Deondre eventually left.

We'd always run back into each other somewhere and agree to try again but he always wanted sex, and when I wouldn't put out he would leave.

I started working part-time at a grocery store. One day a guy walks in and locks eyes with me. He's short, thicker than I preferred, but clean cut and looked like he had a real 9-5. He walked in and got a box of cereal and came over to my line on the opposite side of where he came in. He began to chit-chat with me. Something was very different about him.

He's saying little things, and I'm laughing. He just looks at me straight-faced as if nothing is funny. Then he says, "I'm Anton, can I call you sometime?"

"You're lucky you're funny," I tease. "If I give you my number can you promise me one thing?"

"What," he asks.

"Promise me you won't call every day."

He gives me a strange look.

"Promise me," I insisted.

"Ok I promise," he says, and I give him my number.

He calls not too often but often enough. When he does, we don't' talk about much, and he never asks to take me out. He was moving way too slow, even for this wannabe church girl.

Eventually, I run back into Deondre and I let Anton know I'm getting back with my ex.

Deondre and I get back together, and this time he takes me out of town. We go to Hilton Head Island. We bathed together and still, I gave him none. We went out to dinner that night, and he says, "I guess I'll order the fish since that's as close as I'm going to get to any."

I let tears well up in my eyes, and one lone teardrop fell.

"No, nooo I was playing. It's ok," he panics. "Don't do that, don't cry."

You already know my tears were just for show.

I figured out pretty early that if you fuss at a guy, a lot of times they don't hear you, but if you act really hurt it makes them feel like shit.

A power move!

Deondre and I lasted for about two months before he again announces, "I'm out."

He left, and I decided to call Anton.

We talked a little while, but it was still more of the same. He was always saying he would be out of town for a few weeks and I would hardly see him. Things weren't going anywhere.

One day mom and I were driving, and we pulled up right beside a motorcycle. I was checking the guy out. He turns his head towards me to check me out, and all we could do was bust out laughing. It was Deondre; we waved, and he pulled off.

Not too long after that, I came home to a note on the door. Deondre says he has to talk to me. I was a little worried about calling him; *what would he possibly need to talk about?* I called anyway, and he's saying how bad he misses me, and he's ready to be with me *for real.*

We get back together and finally I give in and we *get it on,* and I've never known sex until I began sleeping with Deondre.

By this time my mom and I had moved into a trailer park. She and my dad had filed for and finalized their divorce.

While with Deondre I'd began battling an old demon, bulimia. I would rotate between starving myself and bulimia by vomiting and drinking Milk of Magnesia and Magnesium Citrate.

While living with my sister, I'd worked at a restaurant where I met a white coworker who had lost a lot of weight. I asked her how and she told me about this prescription that was basically *speed.* I asked her for some. She agreed and warned me that the meds were powerful.

She was right! I was bouncing all around the restaurant. I had so much energy I actually worked that night.

I asked my doctor for a prescription for the amphetamine and needless to say, she gave me the stink eye and said she wouldn't be prescribing me *any* drugs. She said what she would be willing to do is prescribe me with an antidepressant. I told her about my back pains, and it turned out I'd gotten a kidney infection from the overuse of magnesium products. She informed me that we needed to treat my depression first and worry about weight later.

Turns out she was right; my life was about to take a dramatic turn.

I'm a huge sleeper already, but suddenly, I was tired ALL of the time.

I dropped out of school because I was falling asleep driving. I put blankets over the windows in my room, so it was pitch black. All I did was sleep and eat.

Slowly I began to say whatever was on my mind. I became even more of a hypochondriac, and my OCD was on full throttle. My mom had no clue what to think, let alone what to do. I somehow adjusted to the medication

I was given, and eventually, I began to sleep on a more regular schedule.

Eventually, I moved into a studio apartment by myself.

I'd entertained a few chicks here and there that I'd met online. So, I figured now that I was living on my own I'd meet another one just for fun.

That's how I met Monica.

Monica was one of those girls who didn't know how cute she was, so she settled for anything. She was very shapely and, in my opinion, spent way more time grooming than she needed. She was irritating.

She lived another town over. I'd gone to her town to see her maybe once or twice. On one occasion, we met up and decided to fool around. I fondled her breasts. We kissed and during the process her shirt comes off. I remember asking if she'd had a baby because she had loose stretch marks.

"No," she says. "I just used to be very heavy."

She wasn't small now, maybe average.

"Oh," I said and shrugged. "It's ok."

She ended up giving me oral. It was cool, nothing to rant and rave over. We kept in touch.

Turns out Monica's home life was not the best, so it was easy for me to convince her to come live with me. I drove to her town, packed her up and moved her into my studio apartment. I had only a twin bed myself, so I made it a trundle bed by sliding an extra twin mattress under my bed to be pulled out at bedtime. Honestly, I just liked having her sleep below me next to my bed. I felt like I had a human pet.

A power move.

Sometimes she would try to engage, but I didn't want it.

She'd told me about one of her friends she'd slept with before. I told her to see if she wanted to come *hang out*. I asked her if she had any more girls she could bring to the party. We could only get the one. We went to pick her up from the next town and brought her back to our place.

Monica's friend Kameela was cute, but plain. She was also *super* plus sized, and light skinned. That's usually my type anyway. I like people who are as similar to me as possible. I've never figured that part out. Let's just say, if I were a narcissist, it could actually make sense.

Anyway, we get to the house and start to have girl talk, and I look at Monica to give her the eye, letting her know that it's time to give me a show.

She lays Kameela down on the trundle. I started to take off her clothes. One thing I seem to like that I don't have are small tits. Kameela was a big girl, but she only had a handful of tits. I began to grope her little perky tits as Monica began to finger her and kiss around the insides of her thighs. Kameela reached for my head to try and kiss me and I shook my head no. I began to lick her nipple, and she looks over at me and says, "You're not new to this."

I smile wickedly and shake my head no.

By now Monica has worked her way to Kameela's clit with her tongue. Kameela's eyes roll back, and I reach down to start playing with her ass.

"No," she says. "I've never done that."

"Hush," I whisper to her. The best part for me is hearing them say no. It does something to me for someone to not want me to do something, and my little secret is that I'm going to do it anyway. I push my finger in her tight asshole. She was right; she had never done it.

As I gently push in, she's saying, "Ok, ok no, no stop."

Again I ssshhh her and go in a little deeper. She begins to relax and is actually starting to enjoy it. Monica brings her to climax.

Monica says, "Let me do you now Morgan."

"No," I replied.

She looked at Kameela disappointed at the rejection. Kameela then says, "Can I then?"

"Ok," I replied.

Monica looked a bit jealous but got over it once Kameela began. I'd looked up to watch Kameela sucking my clit and saw Monica smiling as she watched. I held Kameela's head as my nut came to a close.

"My butt is sore," Kameela stated.

"Don't worry," Monica reassured her. "That won't last long. Eventually, it won't even hurt to do it. I actually like it."

Kameela giggled.

I *knew* that Monica wanted an invitation to be pleased next. So, I told her to come and lay beside to me.

Without having to tell her, Kameela knelt her big yellow ass down in front of Monica's pussy and begin to lap it up like a cat lapping milk. I put my finger in Monica's ass and yep, something *had* been there before. She acts like she's just so into it. She's moaning and twisting on her nipples. I push two fingers in, and she begins to move her hips and grind Kameela's face.

I got bored and stopped.

Monica looked up at me disappointed.

"I've gotta go use the bathroom," I offered.

Kameela stayed between Monica's legs until she finished her up.

Truthfully, I was turned off. First of all, Monica was now an old toy, and I was bored with her anyway.

Secondly, as I just said I like resistance. I like to fight you and force you to give me what I want. Having it given to me freely *and* enjoying it was a major turn off.

There are some drawbacks to seeking power. Sometimes, you can't enjoy things that could be enjoyable.

After throwing away the gloves I'd used, I came back and said, "Now you guys scissor."

Monica looked at Kameela, and Kameela said, "No. I don't like that."

"Yeah - no," Monica agreed.

I guess something happened once with Kameela and this position. So, I pushed, "What if I pay you guys $50."

They still said no. I began to caress Kameela and plant gentle kisses on her face and neck. She smiled, continued to resist me and said, "No."

It was two of them, and their loyalty clearly lay with each other. They won that night, but I knew I'd try another day.

But unfortunately, that day never came.

Not only did I not see Kameela again, but I also never had the chance to meet any more of Monica's friends.

I'd started treating Monica poorly. I was snappy and nothing she could do pleased me. I was her only means of transportation and money for a while, and I liked that. That way I could control her.

He who holds the money, holds the power.

Monica ate *when* I fed her and *what* I fed her. I tried to keep her from getting a job so I could keep the control.

But she eventually did.

One day we were arguing about something while I drove her to work. I pulled over. "Get out," I ordered. "Find your own way to work."

She cries but gets out and walks inside of a business, I suppose to call a coworker to come get her. I park the car, get out, and follow her inside demanding my key from her key ring.

We begin struggling over the key ring, and I eventually take it and take my key off. As I'm leaving, she follows me back outside.

I still had the car running and tried to get in on the driver side before she gets to the car, but she gets there quick enough to get in and close the door. I walk around to the other side to get in, and as I sit down, she leaned over and grabbed my keys from the ignition.

I snapped.

I had a pen in my hand, and all I could do was stare at her neck imagining how cool it would be to see blood spurting from it. I take the pen and stab at her neck as hard as I can.

Another situation not well thought out.

Pen pieces fly everywhere, not blood, just the pen. There was my signature on her neck, but no puncture wounds, not even a little one.

What would *you* do if someone had just done that and *you* had the advantage?

Yep, she thought the same thing and commenced to beating my ass. I was lying on my back in the front seat now kicking for dear life. None of them landed. I didn't feel any pain, but her ring left a mark on my forehead. There weren't too many other signs of a tussle.

So, I was good.

She went into the building to again call for help, and I went to work.

Later, I tried to convince her to stay so that we could work it out, but she was out. I asked her to leave her laptop so I could use it and she did. I called her one day to tell her my driver would be bringing it back to her because roaches were coming out of it. She sucked her teeth *knowing* she'd brought them with her.

My "driver" was Matt, the guy who'd given me the gun.

Matt now had a key to my apartment, and my home was his home away from home. He also had a wife, so I was his escape.

I would let him give me oral, but I'd only had sex with him once or twice.

We were very close.

Matt asked me about Monica. "What's up with your girl Monica? I've never known you to let a chick get under your skin."

Because we were close, Matt knew me better than most. He was right. Monica had gotten under my skin. I was irritated that she'd been strong enough to leave when I'd wanted her to stay. Somehow, I knew I wasn't done with her. I let it go for now, but one day, I'd get my revenge.

CONFESSION SIX:

Transference

"Someone has to pay for that."

After the birth of my son, I decided to dedicate ten years of my life to him. I didn't go out, date, or really think much about a social life. I was focused on him; so much so, that I was almost a Mormon.

Denying a thing is not the same as owning it. When you own something, you acknowledge it and then you can possibly move on from it. But when you are in denial, whatever it is that you're denying, only festers and rots and waits for the perfect time to be exposed.

Denial is simply a lie and like all lies, eventually the truth surfaces. I was hurting and embarrassed by what I considered to be a weakness.

Someone (other than myself) had to pay for my pain.

Carmen seemed just as good as anyone.

Carmen was a chick I met through work. She was Hispanic, petite, loud and very ghetto. I didn't want to get too close to her because she was a bit wilder than I wanted to be as a mother.

Eventually, my desires overpowered me, and I began to hang out with her.

In an effort to remain committed to my 'Mormon lifestyle,' I attempted, without success, to introduce Carmen to a higher class of men. I figured if I could tame her, then I could also tame my own thirsts.

It is true that you can't teach old dogs new tricks. What can I say, the chick was a *ho*, so I had to treat her like the *ho* she was.

I needed release one day and found my victim on a social networking site. To gain her trust, I had to talk to her for a few days, you know, put in work.

"I can tell that you're curious about women," I said confidently.

"Wow," she seemed impressed. "How do you know that?"

"I just have a sense about these things," I was kind of already bored. Instinctively I knew that she wouldn't present any *real* challenge or resistance. However, I continued to tell her whatever I knew she wanted to hear.

"Would you like to go with me to my girl Carmen's house and chill with us," I asked.

"Sure," she agreed right away. "What's on the agenda?"

"Just a smoke and chill session," I responded.

Now my girl Carmen's house was straight nasty, but I wasn't a*bout* to bring this shit to *my* home.

We arrived at my girl Carmen's house and made ourselves comfortable. Carmen got up and conveniently goes to the bathroom while I seized the moment to seduce this chick aggressively. She was a little hesitant until I started licking her already hard nipple.

I can tell she wants it but isn't totally comfortable yet. She hears my girl come out of the bathroom and quickly tried to cover up.

"Don't' worry about her," I whispered in her ear. "It's just you and me."

I yank off her clothes, and me and Carmen lick her breasts until she totally relaxes.

I sit up to put gloves on while she looks at me questioningly and instinctively closes her legs. I wasn't going to lose any ground with this chick, so I spread them back open and smack the inside of her thigh. She didn't like it, but I gave her a threatening look that said, "I wish you would say something."

With power, comes punishment and with punishment, comes reward, so I began to massage between her legs until she's wet enough for me to insert two fingers. I bite her nipple, and again I can tell it hurts, but who cares this is for me, not her.

I didn't bring her here to pleasure her.

I jammed three fingers in her pussy and my pinky in her ass. She kind of likes it but is letting me know that's her limit. I motion Carmen to come get in between her legs.

Carmen comes over and starts kissing the chick's inner thighs, and the chick likes *that* a lot. She's moaning and grinding her hips at the thought of my girl sucking her pussy.

She relaxes enough for me to figure I'd try jamming two fingers in her ass.

"Ouch," she complains. "I've never done anything like this before."

I'm not listening, and it doesn't seem like the fingers will go in without her jumping up, so I go back to trying four fingers in her pussy.

She's distracted.

Carmen has arranged herself so that the chick can finger her. I can tell she's loving putting her fingers in my girl Carmen's wet pussy.

Even though she's distracted, she keeps shooting me looks as I continue trying to cram my four fingers inside her tight pussy. She was tight, not the tightest, but certainly tighter than my girl Carmen's loose ass pussy.

Eventually, I realized my four fingers weren't going to fit. Now I was bored.

I took off my gloves and stood up. The party was over. Now it was time to do what I'd come here to do.

Dominate.

"Get up," I ordered. "You can leave."

Carmen wasn't stressed about it. She was used to me by now and knew enough not to argue. She simply pulled up her pants from her knees and left the room. The chick, on the other hand, was clearly confused.

"What's the matter," she asked. "Did I do something wrong?"

I could tell she was beginning to feel what I'd hoped she'd feel, embarrassed.

Yeah, I would have been happier if the two of them had gone at it more, but for some reason, my *ho* ass friend decided to have standards *that* day. Maybe it was because I'd basically just brought this girl in from off the street.

Either way, the cherry on top was when she was laying there totally exposed and naked and realized not only was it over, but none of *my* clothes had ever come off.

Pain and humiliation *transferred*.

I was satisfied.

CHAPTER SIX: A TETHER
Someone To Be There

The police were looking for me for various reasons, old parking tickets, bench warrants for failure to appear, and vehicular manslaughter. I wasn't worried as much as I was irritated at the interruption. I went to my aunt's job to talk to her and her lawyer friend about my troubles with the law.

My cousin Tonya works there too. We weren't as close anymore. Ever since I'd gotten saved, even though she had too and was also Holy Ghost filled, I could just see her even better now. I wasn't feeling her anymore. I loved her but didn't like her. I didn't show it. I still came when she called and kept in touch, but I wasn't up under her anymore.

"Don't tell Tonya my business Aunt Becca," I said to her. "She always talks about you behind your back and tells everyone that will listen, all of your business. She's not going to do me like she does you."

Aunt Becca's loyalty to Tonya wouldn't let her take what I said to heart.

Meantime, I felt like I was going crazy, so I needed a tether. My mom and I talked a lot, and I think she understood me better than anyone, but she would ask questions. She'd want me to try and make sense of things, and that was just too hard for me. I needed someone to hold on to, someone who knew me well, that I could run to, someone who wouldn't make demands on me. I just needed someone to *be there.*

I couldn't help but think of Steven.

Steven used to say that I tried to force him to have sex with me. I don't believe it or remember it, but then again, this *is* me we're talking about.

There was one time I remember of fooling around, him bending me over, but things didn't go like I thought they would.

When Steven and I were kids, we used to do things to keep us from having too much sex since as Christians, it was wrong. Steven would slide his penis between my pussy lips, much like a hot dog in a bun, and instinctively I knew to hold the underside with my hand and jack him off at the same time. He's always been an easy nut. A lot of times we didn't even have to take our clothes off. I'd just back my butt up to the front of his jeans and grind on him.

He'd be like, "Red stop! Stop it," because he knew it was only a matter of time before he'd bust all over his clothes. He'd often have to run home and change and come back.

This day, however, he didn't bust. He pushed me off of him and said, "I can't, I just can't. I'm not right."

We didn't talk a whole lot after that, but we kept in touch.

Anyway, like I said, a lot was going on financially and I could no longer afford to live alone. I'd asked Deondre a few times if I could move in with him. The answer was always no. I was furious. But I called him over to help me start getting rid of things at my studio apartment so that I could move.

"Where did you decide to move," he asked.

"To a really cheap and bad part of town," I said smartly. "I'm not telling you where I'm moving. If you don't care enough to let me move with you, then you don't care enough to know where I'm going. Just know if I die over there or get raped it's on your hands. Plus, I have a new friend anyway. I'll see if he can help take care of me."

"What, who," he asked clearly upset. "What friend?"

"Don't worry about it," I said carelessly. "For someone who doesn't care you got a whole lot of questions."

"Look whoever it is," he begins as he leans against my body and pushes me against his truck. "You tell him to get missing, daddy's back, and you're coming home with me." He kisses and presses his dick against me.

Whenever Deondre's around me, his dick is hard. He's well-endowed too, so I knew I had the upper hand the minute he stepped out his truck and walked over to me.

One day I'd pulled up in my car to where he was, he came walking over, and I could just see his dick rising. I'm like, "Deondre, is that all I am to you?"

"No baby, of course not," he tried to reassure me. "It's just when he sees you he knows how we be getting it in, so it makes him happy. Look at him; I could poke a hole in your car door right now."

Clearly, nothing had changed.

"You mean it, Deondre?" I asked full of excitement. "I can move in?"

"Yeah," he said. "But get rid of your friend. I mean it."

"Ok," I said already wondering if I meant it.

CONFESSION SEVEN:

Ma, Are You Sick?

---

*"I haven't worked out who is who yet, but
I'm definitely not alone."*

"Ma? Are you sick?"

"No, I'm fine why would you ask that?" I asked as I turn the wheel to make a right, heading to my sister's house.

"No, I mean sick as in the head," my son repeated. "Are you sick in the head."

I looked back at my beautiful baby boy. Sometimes, he favored me, but most of the time he was the spitting image of his dad, except he had lots of dark curly hair.

"Have I done anything to make you think that?" I asked suddenly fearful of where this question came from. "I don't quite understand."

"Ma, just are you," Elijah asked in frustration. "You know, like I've heard you say people are sick in the head."

"If anything indicated I'm sick in the head, it would be that I don't beat you like I should," I laughed. "You're rotten, and I don't beat you enough, so yeah I probably am sick."

Elijah was only eleven, and already he was insightful. His piercing gray eyes seem to be able to see into my soul. He was asking me questions that I didn't have the answer to. So, I tried to keep it light and make him laugh, but he wasn't trying to go there.

"You make up things that aren't real and try to make it seem like it's someone else when it's really you," he said wise beyond his years. "Like Aunties, they're acting like it's the kids and always hollering, but really it's them."

It made me feel a little better hearing him say it *that* way. It would devastate me to know that Elijah knew more about my actual sickness than he did. Even though he had no idea of the depth of my demons, his question still took me to a sunken place.

One of my biggest fears was that one day he would sit me down and say, "Mom, it *was* you. You *were* the monster I needed protecting from. You made it seem like you were isolating me from all these bad and sick monsters in the world. People are actually good, but no one could protect me from you. You did all these horrible things to me and tried to convince me that others were trying to do them to me."

And the worst part would be that I wouldn't even remember or realize I had done any of them.

I have moments like that. Moments when my mind plays tricks. Some parts of my life already seem like they're missing. I've been in and out of depression and on and off mind-altering medicines so much; I sometimes have a hard time believing what's real and what isn't.

Once I was changing my son's bedding, and his mattress looked horrible. I had just bought it maybe five or six years ago.

I'm so overprotective of him in many ways, yet I'm failing him in almost every way. I couldn't even remember the last time I had changed his bedding and could probably count on one hand how many times I actually had in the five or six years since I bought the mattresses. Which explained why the mattress looked horrible.

It made me sick to my stomach. I couldn't tell what the stains were. Blood? Pee? I hadn't known about him peeing or having nosebleeds but a few times. The amount seemed almost too much to be blood, but it was dark.

Of course, my mind raced in all sorts of directions.

What kind of mother are you?

How can your child's bed look like this and you not know? Have you abused your own child and forgotten? Your son deserves better.

I had to make the voices shut up, and I had to just move on. Sometimes, it was more than the voices that were disruptive.

One morning Elijah and I were backing out of the driveway

"The tailgate is open," I tell him pointing at the indicator light on the dash.

"Want me to close it?" Elijah says.

"Sure," I said.

As he's back there smiling happily at the chore, I realized the car was still in reverse.

Morgan says, "OMG, be careful don't make any moves. Don't accidentally run over my baby."

Sometimes the voice is a he, other times it's a she. I haven't worked out who is who yet, but I'm definitely not alone.

Today, the voice was a male voice.

"This is your opportunity," he says. "It could look just like an accident. Put him out of his misery. He's young enough to get into heaven without having to answer for his life. You have to do it fast and hard though. You want to make sure he's gone, not mangled for the rest of his life."

Of course, I quickly dismissed the voice, but I recognized that it was not my own. I was thankful when Elijah got back in the car.

CHAPTER SEVEN: INTUITION
Suspect

I moved in with Deondre, and I'm as happy as a basic broad could be. Guess what though? I don't have much money because I only work part-time. Deondre is not having it. So, even though I'm trying to help out around the house, everything annoys him. I wash his clothes, and he asks if I could please NOT do his laundry.

He also had to fix a few things I'd broken around his house. Yeah, he was getting pretty fed up with me.

Finally, I got a job at a pet store where they said they'd train me and I could make up to $1,000 a week. I was excited and told Deondre. He just laughed at how naive I was.

Deondre didn't take me seriously at all. He was seven years older than I and already paying a mortgage and trying to do big things. He couldn't take any more of me, and after living there for only a month and a half, he informed me I had to go.

To add insult to injury, he also told me that in the meantime I had to sleep in the other bedroom on the blow-up mattress.

Really?!

One night bored, I was at work and decided to go to Wal-Mart to buy a watch with an alarm so that I could go to sleep at work. I worked the 3rd shift as a part-time gig, so it'd be ok.

I started walking around the store looking at things to kill time and what do you know, I ran into Anton, I hadn't seen him in about two years.

"Hey," I said to him.

He looks up from the box he's working on and says, "Oh hey, how are you doing?"

I said, "I'm fine. I hope you are."

After chit chatting a little longer, he asks, "Whatever happened to us? Why didn't we work out?"

"You moved too slow," I replied. "We never even went on any dates."

"Do you think I'd move that slow now?"

"I don't know."

"Well give me your number again," he pressed. "and let's find out."

We started talking.

One night, Deondre was gone, so I decided to call Anton from the house phone. There was no answer, I hung up and laid down to sleep.

Later when Deondre comes home, the phone rings. He comes into my room and asks, "Did you call somebody?"

"Yeah," I said matter-of-factly.

"Well he's on the phone," he says gruffly and shoves the phone at me. "Here."

I took the phone and had to immediately explain to Anton what was going on. He said it was ok and he'd stick by me while I was transitioning out. We had a good conversation. I hung up and here comes Deondre.

"Oh really," he spits out angrily. "*That's* how you do? I think you should try to move out as soon as possible; it's just not going to work."

"Ok," I said without feeling. I didn't care. I had someone else to look forward to now.

"Oh, and he sounds like a punk too," Deondre says.

Men can be so petty.

One day while Deondre was gone I decided to pack all my crap and do him a favor. I was backing out of his driveway and making a run for it. Too bad I never did learn how to drive well and ended up right in his ditch in the front yard.

Guess who comes home and has to tow me out?

"That's what you get for trying to sneak and leave," he said.

Anyway, I headed over to my mom's two-bedroom apartment to share a room with my little brother.

It wasn't long before Anton, and I were back at it and pretty much inseparable. One night he even came by and knocked on the window at 3 a.m. He was on the way home and wanted to check on me. I was pretty upset about it and told him so the next day.

"Don't be coming by my mom's house like that."

He agreed, but that was just the beginning of a long, bumpy road.

One day we were at his apartment things got really heated.

"I don't think we should be together anymore," I began. "Things are just too intense."

Proving my point, he stood up and put his hand around my throat and said, "Don't ever tell me you're leaving me again. You're never leaving me, do you hear me, do you hear me?!"

He loosened his grip just enough, so I could say, "Yes."

131

We laid back down and cuddled.

I laid there thinking, *he who holds the money, holds the power.* Anton was taking care of me.

One day, coming home from work the cops pulled me over with warrants for my arrest. I hadn't pulled off the road enough, so they said they had to tow my car to the impound yard.

After the car sat at the impound long enough, I called the dealer to let them know they could pick it up and from where.

Before this, I'd been hiding it so they wouldn't take it. I didn't have the money to get it from the impound nor did I think they'd let me. Both airbags were deployed anyway.

While living with Deondre I was driving home, and the traffic suddenly stopped. I had no insurance, so I yanked the wheel to avoid hitting the car in front of me. I ran off the road and hit the deep ditch so hard I bounced back out of it. I had seething pain all over my entire back. I couldn't move any part of my body. I just knew I was paralyzed.

So yeah, I knew they weren't letting me drive that car off the impound yard.

I was in a bad place and relied on Anton for a lot.

He actually did start to help clean my life up too. He asked for all of my court dates and took me to them to clear everything up.

At some point, Anton was on this kick about us having a baby. He went with me to a doctor's visit and told my doctor he wanted a baby and I needed to come off the meds. I was able to come off, and we started working on a baby. I got pregnant but at my first visit was told it wouldn't survive and it didn't.

Anton pressured me to try again right away, but I didn't want to. I told him to try to get me pregnant, and I'd try not to and whoever wins, wins.

As time went by, somehow, I became the breadwinner. Of course my family, especially my father didn't care for that.

When Deondre's transmission on his truck went out and I was paying the bills and his transportation, my dad was insistent that I leave him.

"He said he loves you and has nothing to hide, but he'll never be able to take care of you. If you start out taking care of him, you'll end up taking care of him forever. Let him go," he warned. "A real man will get himself together and come back for you."

What can I say, this man had helped me so much, I couldn't abandon him now in his time of need.

I couldn't pay the bills and take care of Deondre so I moved in with my mom. But then she kicked me out because she was getting married.

"You're twenty-five now for heaven's sake," my mom said. "It's time."

Oh, I gave my mom the business and told her I wouldn't be at the wedding. For days, I remember sitting in the living room on the couch crying and crying.

I moved in with my dad and he did his best to help me. He would ask me questions to try and understand what was wrong. I didn't want to live with him, and in my mind, my mom was a traitor for making me.

Dad told me life would get better and he tried to make it better.

"What type of car do you want," he asked me one day.

"There isn't a car I want," I said sullenly. "There's nothing in life I have a want for. I'm just here waiting to die. We all are. What's the use of having wants or obtaining your wants? Nothing is real but the afterlife. We're all in one big waiting room, and everything around us is just to distract us until our number is called."

I remember him nodding his head and looking as if he was just not going to touch that at all. We sat and watched TV in silence, except for my sniffles and nose blowing.

A little less than a year after the miscarriage I was pregnant again. I eventually left dads' place to live with my sister.

At six months pregnant, I finally got my own apartment. I had to threaten Deondre to get him to move in with me.

I'm like, "What the fuck, you beg me to have this baby and you trying to leave already?"

He moved in, and things just changed.

I'd bought a little old car for $450. I loved that old rust bucket. It was fast with a rebuilt engine.

Deondre used it now to drive me around until I got my license back. I did, and I began to do so well. I financed us a mini-van just in time for the baby's arrival.

Well actually if you let my mom tell the story, I tricked her into buying me a mini-van.

She'd had some sort of surgery and was high on meds. I asked her to co-sign, and she agreed. However, when the guy came by her house for her signature, since she was immobile at the time, he had her sign the buyer spot and I the cosigner. I kept her credit pristine though.

The day I went to deliver, Deondre and I got into a huge fight. He pushed me, and I landed on the bed and bounced onto the floor. It didn't stop there. He came at me, and I picked up a curtain rod and tried to hit him with it. He blocked it and was still coming towards me. Somehow my pinky nail caught his arm over his bicep and ripped about four inches of flesh open. It was a good thing too because he was coming in for the kill. I think he was going to hit me that day. He never had, but he had been violent.

Later, after Deondre got stitched up, we delivered the most beautiful little boy I'd ever seen in my life, Elijah.

And my life changed forever.

Having a baby didn't stop our fighting and after about two years of putting up with Deondre's bullshit, I knew I had to go.

We were arguing one night on the phone. He was all stirred up about something, and I could hear the warning in his voice. I needed to get away. I hung up the phone and put something against the front door to hold him off as I packed up some things the baby and I needed.

He was closer to home than I'd anticipated. He tried opening the door, and when it wouldn't open because of the barricade, he hulked out. He kicked the door in ruining the door frame.

(I ended up staying in that apartment for two more months with a broken door, anyone could have walked in. I was too ashamed to have maintenance fix it.)

Finally, I'd had enough. I alerted my mom and put a plan into action. Whenever I noticed his eyes switch over, I'd speed dial, my mom. Having her on the phone calmed him down.

I told him I was moving, and he couldn't come with me. His big, badass cried like a fucking baby. For some dumb reason, I felt bad, but put my two fingers up anyway.

Before I moved out, I'd run into, yes you guessed it, Anton. We were back in touch.

After moving into my new place, Anton and I were able to keep in touch a bit more. I wasn't interested in a relationship because I had a child now, but I did like having him around.

God would tell me now more than ever before to stop messing with Anton, but I just couldn't and couldn't figure out why.

One day Anton wanted to move in for a bit while he fixed his money issues. I'd been knowing him at this point for more than seven years now. I trusted him and don't forget; I loved him. So sure, I let him move in.

On one of the first days he moved in, he came home from work and asked me to run to Subway and get him a sandwich.

"No," I said shaking my head. "My baby is already in the bed. I'm not getting him up to get you a sandwich."

"Just leave him here," he said. "I'm about to take my shower anyway."

"No," I said still shaking my head. "I'm not leaving my baby with you. I'll make you a sandwich."

"What do you mean you're not leaving him with me," he said with an attitude. "Ok, just wait until you need me to babysit, I'm going to say no."

"Ok, first of all," I said now with my own attitude. "I will *never* ask you to babysit my baby, *ever*. Now, do you want me to make you a sandwich or are you going back out."

"Yeah, just make me one," he says with a growing attitude.

Now ladies, I'm a smart cookie, but not smart enough.

Some of you don't get it at all and even after I point everything out, you still won't. If I can help anybody do one thing, I'm hoping it will be to help you all watch your kid and keep them from sneaky people.

Why the fuck does a hungry man drive past multiple Subways to come home and ask *me* to leave *my* house and *my* baby to go back out and get *his* fat ass a sandwich?

I put this in Anton's file as *suspicious*.

As time went on, things just weren't adding up.

You know that light sleeping thing we moms do? Well, I had it, and out of the blue, I'd wake up, and this nigga would be coming back from down the hall *checking* to see if he left clothes in the dryer.

What the hell?

Suspect.

I woke up once to see his shadow standing in the bathroom like he was listening to see if I was awake or not. Then he resorted to sleeping on the floor because his back hurt, but I think it was him trying not to wake me as he was sneaking out of bed.

He worked late and would come home around 3 am. He had a key, but I would bolt the door at night so that it required me to wake up and let him in. It had gotten to the point, that once he was home, I didn't sleep. I couldn't figure it out, but I was *very* uncomfortable.

He told me to stop bolting the door, so I didn't have to wake up to let him in. I informed him it was no bother at all. I'd started sprinkling small toys around my son's bed so if he was going in there sneaking it would murder his feet.

One day we were talking, and he looked over my shoulder towards my son's room.

I slowly turned my head to see what he was looking at.

I had rigged a jump rope across the door to trip his fat ass if he went in there at night. Surely, he couldn't see that from here.

There was never any sign he'd ever gone in. I can only pray he never touched my baby. He moved out after having lived there only a month and a half. My whole taste for him disappeared. I no longer wanted him the way I did.

Ladies, our intuition is in place for a reason.

We may not be able to figure it out, but if it feels wrong, then go ahead and consider that it is wrong. If you suddenly become very overprotective of your child around someone, your intuition is saying there is a threat to your child. I wish I'd known earlier and followed my intuition without question.

You live and learn.

Some people may think I'm crazy, but statistics don't lie. 6 or 7 out of 10 children are molested before they turn 18.

That's a lot of kids.

Long ago, before I even had a child, Oprah said that no one deserves the benefit of the doubt when it comes to your kids.

I recently found out that four different people molested Tyler Perry, one being a woman, all before age 10.

Our kids are in shark-infested waters, and they are the flavor of the day. You had better suspect everyone you know.

I'd rather act crazy than be stupid.

There is no benefit in doubt. We too often doubt ourselves and trust others with our most precious gems.

This was one time where my need for power and control served me and my baby.

CONFESSION EIGHT:

It Hurts

"I don't deal with you anymore God. I just really don't."

I was beginning to get burned out from my career and decided to head back to school.

For most of my son's younger years, he was with his dad. I knew how to make money, but I was never any good at doing the domestic, stereotypical stuff that women are expected to do like cleaning the house or cooking.

But my son's father seemed better at it. He even seemed to enjoy it. He took care of my son better than me anyway, so I became 'the man of the house.'

I would work all day, run home to visit my baby, and then head back out to go to school. I was working six days a week and in school five nights a week.

I was a pet stylist and believe it or not it's hard and stressful. They would overbook me often. I became known as the bad dog lady because I was good with them; which means I got them a lot. Most days I'd work without food, drink or a restroom break. People are crazy about their dogs.

Although I'm not concerned with the feelings of others, I still consider myself a people pleaser. I know it doesn't make sense, but my life doesn't make sense. How do you explain the need to help people and yet desire to tear them apart? That was the paradox that I called my life.

I just couldn't take breaks knowing I had so much work waiting on me. I'm also impatient and like to get things done quickly.

So I'm going through all of this, in pain and dealing with what I called a big, huge, white, work bully. I think she was upset that I was doing well in life. She'd always say I know you're leaving us once you get your license. I really wasn't thinking of it. I loved my job but wanted supplemental income, so I could continue loving it and not *have* to work so hard.

One day I'd read a disturbing text over my mom's shoulder and said, "I'm putting a stop to this today."

As I'm leaving, she says, "Well while you're on the way to where you're going think about which one of us you want to raise Elijah while you're in jail."

"No one says I'm doing anything illegal," I holler over my shoulder.

My mom knew me all too well.

I called up my boy Dwayne and told him I needed someone beat within inches of their life. I said, "Cut out his tongue, poke out his eardrums, and bring his eyes back to me on toothpicks. I want them in my margarita. If you do all of that, there's no way he can identify you."

"Look Red," Dwayne said. "I can go give him a *regular* beat down with my boys. We'll put him in the hospital but all that sick shit you have to do yourself. If you want his eyeballs, you have to come get them."

We tried several times to see how we could get to this guy who was living in another state and working on a military base. We couldn't see around it. Again, thank God things could not go the way I wanted them to go.

Instead, I started praying and getting my life together and waited for an answer from God. God told me to get in line and live right so I could hear Him. He said, "When I say time, I want you to go."

The next time I was at my mom's house I caught wind of something else that happened, and I heard God say GO!

I left my mom's quietly and as if everything was normal. I alerted the authorities for them to handle it and prayed and waited. It took several stressful months to conclude. Meanwhile, people were in danger, and it was nothing I could do but wait.

During the stress of that, my grandmother passed.

One day my son's father asked me if I'd seen her.

"No," I replied.

"I think you need to see her; she looks sick."

I snapped at him, "Why would you say something like that? You're so stupid! No one has said anything to me about anything."

He knew, and I knew he knew, but I didn't want to hear it. He would pick my son up from over there, so he saw her more than I did. He loved my grandma. Who didn't? Shortly after that, she was gone.

I finished school and started working on my own business, so I could now be a mother to my child.

I realized those were the years he would remember, and I wanted him to enjoy them with me. I was always so tired before that when I did see him, I was snappy.

One day as we were riding he says something that was finally the last straw. I tapped out on life.

Elijah had an experience with another kid who was quite a bit older and female. It wasn't as bad as it could have been, but it crushed me.

God are you serious?! The ONE thing I say do not touch. Seriously?! I can't deal with you anymore God. I just really can't.

Ok, that sounds stupid. I'm sorry, but really?!

I kept calm for my child, and I didn't ask too many questions. The next day I started looking into getting us help. I did alert the parents of the other child, but that's not my business to tell what happened over there.

I took my child to counseling.

There were days he cried, and days he was angry. Often I had to drive with one hand as my other hand reached back to hold his.

"Mom I had a dream about a woman last night, and she had perfect breasts," he said as he cried.

"Ok, well guys dream about women all the time. It's going to happen a lot over the years. How does that dream make you feel? Why are you crying?"

"I'm not upset that I had the dream, I'm upset that I have to tell you about it."

"It's ok, thank you for sharing that with Mommy. You can always talk to Mommy about anything. Don't ever feel like you can't."

My baby was feeling ashamed.

It hurt me so bad. At five, my baby shouldn't know this kind of shame. What hurt even more, is that I didn't have the family support like I felt I needed. Who can you tell? Plus, that was my son's business. What if he didn't want anyone to know?

So, it was mostly a secret struggle.

I really tried to hold it together as much as possible, but finally, the stress overtook me. I just couldn't take life anymore. My son's father had to move in. I couldn't get out of bed for anything.

One day I called my mom. I was crying and crying. I said, "Mom, no need to come here, but I need you to pray. I'm not feeling well."

"What's wrong?"

"I don't know."

"What hurts?"

"Everything," I said crying. "I don't know."

"Is it your head? Do you have a cold?"

"I don't know. No, it's not like that," I said frantically. I knew I sounded crazy. "I don't know what's wrong I'm just sick."

"Where's Elijah?"

"In his room, Anton is fixing him dinner."

"Oh, Anton is there," she asked surprised. "Let me speak to him."

They get on the phone and mom is asking questions, and they're just talking. I hear him say, "She just won't get up. She just lays there and cries nonstop."

The next thing I know my mom shows up and prays. She prays for me and everything and everybody right down to my yelping dog that I'm very close to killing.

This is what it looks like when you lose control.

CHAPTER EIGHT: EXTRAS IN THE MORGAN SHOW
Chilled to The Point of Forgetting

I met Desmond at the school where I attended my junior year of high school. We were really good buddies back in the day. He had always claimed to be in love with me.

He found me on Facebook, and we started hanging out.

"I've been looking for you for years," he confessed. "I went back to your house, and your dad would not give me your number. He wouldn't even take mine."

"Yeah," I laughed. "That's my dad for you."

"So, you're not seeing anyone?"

"No."

"Why?"

"I have a secret," I said enjoying his growing suspicion. "You have to promise you won't tell anyone."

"You already know I won't," he said sincerely. "I mean, I love you. I don't think you even realize-"

"I have AIDS," I said cutting him off.

"Really?" He asked wide-eyed.

"Yeah," I said frankly.

"Well, it's ok because I'd die for you," he said, and I knew he meant it. "I mean, not that way. I don't want AIDS, we'd have to use condoms, but I'd take a bullet for you definitely. But I'd take the risk of AIDS for you too."

"Omg, you're so sweet," I said and actually meant it. "I love you too, but nah, I don't have AIDS, but I was born a man."

"Ok, now I know you're lying," he chuckled. "I've known you since high school, and I've felt you up."

"Well, my dick is really little," I explained. "So, it's basically a huge clit. Would you suck it?"

"I don't know, Morgan," sounding very uneasy. "Stop playing."

"Nah but for real, I do have a secret I've never told anybody. So, I've had a wet dream before."

"So," he shrugged. "I have them shits all the time now that we're talking again. Got me nuttin' in my sleep like a damn kid again."

"That's cute, but nah, I'm a girl though. I busted a nut so hard I woke up because my clit was hurting," I said enjoying the sudden look of desire on his face. "I've never even been able to have sex in a dream before much less bust. But guess what I was doing differently this time?"

"What?" He asked, clearly interested.

"I was a man fucking a woman."

"Damn."

"Right, that's some shit, right?"

"Damn," he repeated. "Well you've always been like a dude, so it doesn't surprise me. But I know for a fact you're all woman so really what's up with you being single?"

"For real, for real," I decided to come clean. "I'm waiting until my son gets a little older. Too many creeps out here. I figure once he's around eleven or twelve, I'll be good."

"Nah that's when it's just getting started," he said. "Punk ass pedophiles like them around 10, 11, 12. They start prepping them at the ages before that. I had an uncle like that. The fucked-up shit is everybody in the family knew it and still let him keep kids."

"What? Omg, did it happen to you?"

"Nah, I guess I was too old, I was 14. I'm glad it didn't, but he got my brother and my cousins, and I feel bad I wasn't able to protect them. Come to find out, the family threatened him that he better not do it again. They thought they'd done something. He was still doing it though."

"I'm so sorry to hear that," And I was. "Well, I guess I won't be dating until my baby turns sixteen then."

Later I messaged a friend I'd known since middle school to invite him to my studio.

I proposed to him that I give him free services in exchange for him sending me some high-end clientele.

He agreed, but at the end of our conversation he asked, "Why are you being so professional?"

"What do you mean," I asked very confused.

"You know," he says looking just as confused.

"Oh," I said suddenly aware he was referring to our past. "Well I mean that was a long time ago, and we only hung out like once."

"No," Desmond corrected. "We were best friends. Then you'd go missing, and we'd run into each other in town and be best friends again until you go missing."

Now I'm really worried because that did sound like me. I will go missing on a person *quick.*

A lot of times it's due to boredom.

Anyway, I knew he was telling the truth. *But how? Why don't I remember?*

"You lived in Gladstone Downs. Your house was all the way towards the back of the neighborhood, and it was like a sage green. I would come pick you up, and we'd go hang out. I remember when you lived in Petersburg too. Sometimes I'd say, "I'm on the way," and you'd text back that you'd be in bed and for me to just come in. I had to pass through the living room that had an extra room to the left. The kitchen was off to the right, and I'd walk straight back. Your bathroom was directly in front, at the end of the hallway and to your left was your bedroom. Across from your bedroom was another unoccupied bedroom."

I stared at him as I remembered exactly what homes he was speaking of. However, I didn't remember him ever being at either of them.

"One time you gave me a Jay Z cd," he said.

"See, lies, I don't listen to music."

"Exactly, that's why you gave it to me."

"Omg, I kind of remember. It belonged to someone else. We didn't talk anymore, and he'd left it in my car."

"You were always adamant about not having sex. But we would fool around sometimes, and whenever you were in the mood, you would assist me in getting off somehow. Other times we would just lay and talk and just chill. You've always been so easy to just chill with."

"I think I'm going to be sick. I know you're telling the truth. Other people have told me similar things. Why don't I remember? I need counseling."

"I hate....well maybe it's a good thing.....that I can tell you now. I wish we'd run back into each other sooner, I'm getting married soon. Real soon."

"Congratulations."

"You have a decision to make. I'm being honest with you, so it's your decision whether you want to move forward or not."

"Wait, what do you mean?

"I want you in my life," he said and reached over and touched my thigh.

I get up and move to the other side of the lobby.

Desmond comes over and presses his body against mine. "What are you running for?

"I can't."

"Can't or won't?"

"Both."

He pushes me up against the wall, pinning me between his body and the wall. "I have missed you so much."

"No, nope, nope."

He then rubs between my legs and kisses my neck. "I'm not leaving until it's a yes."

"Oh really?"

"Well at least say you'll see me again."

"You've been here for almost three hours. If it gets you to leave, yes, yes, I will see you again."

People are more like toys to me. I pick them up and put them down when I'm bored. They don't seem real to me.

It's almost like the Truman Show if you've ever seen it. Jim Carey is the star of the movie and he's the only real person in his life. Only he thinks his life is real. But he actually lives on a set.

When he wakes up all of the actors get into place. His wife is an actress, not his real wife. The sun isn't even real, the lights on the set come up just for him. I feel like that most times. Like this is the Morgan Show and everyone around me are just extras.

Things can happen in life sometimes, and I feel like there's some big conspiracy everyone is in on.

For example, like right now I feel I have been blackballed in my town. I feel like word has gotten around that I'm a fraud and the whole town is against me.

When I'm in control, I feel powerful. If I'm not in control, I feel weak. And being weak makes me sick.

CONFESSION NINE:
The Spirit of Love

"Change didn't come easy."

It was a long slow road to recovery.

Along the way I prayed and told God I needed someone. I needed some help. I got on the dating site, Plenty of Fish, and met a lot of people to pass the time.

I didn't even remember my prayer to God until I met Bruce. Bruce was different. I actually enjoyed talking to him. He lived in New York though. We would message about just regular stuff. He wasn't trying to be anything but Bruce.

Eventually, he asked if we could start texting, so we did. One day he says, "Can I call you?"

"I don't know," I said cautiously. "I'm really funny about things. If your voice doesn't sound the way I think it should I'm not going to want to talk to you anymore and I like talking to you."

"Shallow," he says, but then laughs and admits, "I'm the same way."

I agreed to it, and we began talking on the phone.

One day he says, "Why are you always ending our conversations so abruptly? You always have to go."

"I don't want to force things," I explained. "I think it's best to leave while it's still good."

Another day he says, "I like to know what kind of a mother a woman is."

I said, "Well what kind do you think I am?"

He says, "Honestly had you never told me you were one I wouldn't know you were at all. You never talk about him. I never hear him in the background. It's like he doesn't exist."

I'd never really thought about it like that before, but he was right, and it was going to stay that way.

He asks, "Can I come visit one day?"

Again, I informed him that I didn't want to ruin our friendship by seeing him and not liking what I saw. He was persistent, and so eventually I agreed.

We met at Red Lobster. I showed up with a peach, apple pie that I'd baked from scratch for him. I remembered that he'd told me that was his favorite.

It took me a while to get used to looking at him, but once I got comfortable, I knew that I could love him as much as I could love anyone, which wasn't very much.

After dinner, we went to see a movie and ended our night. We continued to keep in touch, and eventually, I decided to let him in on the *real* me.

"I'm sick," I told him. "I take medication for depression."

He says, "It's ok."

I don't let too many people in on that secret for obvious reasons. Bruce responded well, and so I was glad I'd told him.

He came back to visit again, and this time I met him at his hotel. Things were still fairly new, but I was so excited to see him. I let my guard down and became playful.

"Let me show you some of my massage moves," I said forcefully. "Lie on the bed."

I started rubbing his back and said, "This is Swedish."

Then I laid on top of him and said, "This is the full body compression stroke."

"You have to do this to people," He asked.

"Yeah," I reply.

"I don't think I would be able to –"

I interrupt him by getting up on my arms and humping his butt. "And this," I said, "is the booty compression bump."

He laughed so hard he was weak. He tried to roll over and push me, but I had so much strength and energy that I gave him a full workout. I wrestled with him until I saw he *really* could not fight back. Come to find out he smokes too.

"How the fuck are you so strong?" He asks.

I just laugh, and we head out.

We went to PF Changs, and he texted my mother that he was going to marry me one day. (This is something he swears never happened. My mom doesn't remember it either.)

After eating, we went back to his hotel. I start to climb into his bed, and he says, "Don't get into my bed with dirty clothes on."

So, I undress to my bra and panties and get back into the bed.

He says, "And you did it? That's what I'm talking about."

I said, "Look if you touch me just know we go together."

We started to fool around. There was something about him that I couldn't handle. So, I said, "Well, if we ever have sex, then we go together."

I was so afraid because I knew he was someone I could fall madly in love with. I didn't know if I'd ever been in love and I told him that.

He says he hasn't either.

I was already sick. If I fell in love and he left me, I didn't think I could handle that.

After fooling around some more, I head home, and he went back to New York the next day.

We continued to be friends for almost two years. I'd started my business and was whining about how I hated my job and wanted to quit.

Bruce says, "If you quit your job I'll move there and help you with bills."

"No, I can't do that," I said.

Remember, he who controls the money controls the relationship.

Time went on, and I was still sick. Every day was a struggle.

Over the holidays, I left my job and told them that I'd let them know if I would come back.

Two months later, I went back and was still not well. Everything irritated me.

One day they overbooked me by one dog and I lost it. I told them I'd finish that dog, but then I was leaving and not coming back.

To this day I hear they still can't hold a person in that position.

Anyway, I went home and told Bruce I'd done it, I quit. He says, "ok" and immediately started looking for jobs and flying out for interviews. It didn't take him long to find one, and soon he moved in. I moved into the bedroom across from my son and gave him the master.

And just like I warned him I would, I aggravated the shit out of that man. So much that after a month and a half he moved out.

We continued to keep in touch though.

One day I said, "Let's go to the movies."

He said, "Are we meeting and riding together or meeting there or what?"

He purchased the tickets, told me the location and the time. We decided we would meet there.

"Where are you," he was calling from his cell phone.

"On the way," I responded.

"How far are you?"

"Right down the street."

What he didn't know is that I meant right down the street from my house. Bruce was very anal. He was an IT guy. He was very organized and generally speaking, everything I was not. He liked writing lists for any task at hand.

"You were looking at the wrong day," he hissed. "The movie starts later."

By the time I finally get there, he was HOT! His veins were popping out his forehead, and he was grinding his teeth so hard his jawbones were clenched.

I'm like, "Come on lighten up."

But he wasn't trying to hear that. He goes to the bathroom, and I go inside the theater. I waited and waited and waited, but he never showed up.

So, I get up and leave and head for home, crying, of course. Then I think to myself, "You wanted to see that movie, and it's paid for, just go watch it." So, I head back to the theatre and actually enjoy the movie.

I texted him afterward:

Thanks, I enjoyed the movie, too bad you weren't there.

He says:

I came back, but you were gone. So, I left.

Then I say:

You know, if I really upset you that bad then I set you free.

He responded:

For good this time?

Obviously, I'd said I was done with him a few times before. Sounds right. That's my MO. I let him go, but after a few weeks of misery, I tried reaching out to him a number of ways. He'd blocked me on google chat, so I knew I was blocked from emailing him. I tried to anyway. I also called and texted. The numbers had been changed. I was devasted and forced to move on.

About a year later, I ran into some random guy I sort of knew. We exchanged numbers. He began texting me and for some reason, I all of a sudden was no longer able to control my feelings.

This had started with Bruce. He softened me up and now this guy was threatening to make me weak. But I was rebellious; I would give him nothing. He wanted to know why I was so emotionless and expressionless.

I didn't show it outwardly, but the way he made me feel was otherworldly. I knew something else was at play.

Some days I would lie in the fetal position, with a yearning and an ache for this person. I could not understand why though. Finally, he could not take any more of *whatever it was* he couldn't take. I also self-sabotaged things a bit, because I also could no longer take *whatever* was going on.

One night I was awakened by a bright white light at the foot of my bed. I can only describe it as Jesus. He said, "You're taking on a new spirit."

I said, "I don't care what it is, I like it."

I had never had *feelings* like that before. I could *feel* everything, and I was super sensitive. It hurt, but in a good way.

Then another bright white light appeared. It was masculine and huge. Jesus' image appeared smaller and softer. This new figure wasn't angry, but you could tell it was very masculine. It was massive, and I looked in awe as he walked behind the first figure, rounded the edge of my bed and approached me. As he got closer, he got on top of me and rested inside me. I peacefully fell back to sleep.

I can only describe what happened as God giving me the spirit of love. I know all Christians are *supposed* to display love. However, keep in mind, once you give your life to Christ, you do not automatically bear all of the fruits. Some of us have to learn patience, wisdom, and for me, love.

I was definitely softer, but I still had a long way to go.

Later that same year I was approached by a man on my business Facebook page. His name was Vaughn, he was older, distinguished, and seemed settled. I'd promised myself that the next decent man to come along I'd be just your basic broad and go along, to get along. After all, two decent men had walked out, and I was like, "I can't even do this in less than a year."

The thought occurred to me that maybe it was me. Maybe I gave people too hard of a time. Maybe all of those people were actually blessings.

Change didn't come easy.

Vaughn would try and talk to me, and I'd be short as usual. Eventually though, he worked his way in, and we would talk on the phone. I remember him saying, "My birthday is in December, and if you are who I think you are, you have to celebrate it with me in Hawaii."

Two things I love are power and trips.

Still, he asked me out a few times, and I declined.

One day he asked, and I went back and forth. Yes. No. Yes. No. Then finally I said, "Ok. If we're going on this trip I should go ahead and meet you now, so we don't waste time planning for nothing."

I knew I didn't look like my Facebook picture anymore. I'd gained 60 pounds the year I implanted the 5-year birth control device. I'd just taken it out that summer. I was starting to lose weight, but I was still pretty large. I'm a pretty confident woman though, so I wasn't too worried about what he thought.

We met at a restaurant two towns over from me and one town over from him. Upon seeing him, I was not attracted at all. This was nothing new, as I am hardly physically attracted right off anyway. There was also no spiritual connection. It was pretty awkward. He picked up on it and decided to take me to a fancier spot. I'd driven, and he'd Ubered.

Something I would not ordinarily do was date a car-less man.

He tried to ride with me, but I declined and told him I wasn't comfortable with that. He arranged for Uber to come back and since I had never Ubered, I agreed to ride with him.

We head to a nearby mall, and he turns on the charm.

Suddenly he was confident and took charge. Seeing confidence in how he handled himself made me take notice. Now I wanted to see what this guy Vaughn had to offer.

Time passed, and we continued to talk and date. I was sure to mention how spoiled I was and how people were always gifting me and that I hardly had to pay or drive or do anything. I do this when I date to let a guy know what I like.

He was listening.

He bought me gifts. Nice ones. I'm not materialistic, but I like gifts, trinkets. Things I can look at when I'm at home and thinking about memories.

I'd always been this way.

In school when I saw something I liked, especially something a guy had, I'd try to get it. I remember this cutie named Brian who used to wear a Dallas Cowboys puff jacket to school. Every day I'd ask to wear it. At first, he'd say no, but eventually, he knew to hand it over every morning, and I'd return it before going home, not without asking if I could have it.

Again, he'd say no every day until one day he said, "Fine keep it."

I only wore it a few more times. I think it was more about getting him to give in to me than actually having it. I kept it for a long time though. I would look at it and sometimes smell it from time to time.

If you look back at my senior pictures, I'm wearing a male's watch and some bracelets.

I wore my souvenirs proudly.

CHAPTER NINE: SOMETHING JUST AINT RIGHT

His Femininity

It was a struggle dating Vaughn even with the gifts. Something was just not right. He seemed a bit *feminine*.

"I usually don't date churchmen," I'd told him. "If a man is at church and isn't following behind his wife, he's a predator of *some* sort. He's either preying on women, other men or little kids."

I left out money, but money was one too.

He didn't like me being negative that way, but he didn't say much more about it.

I wanted to leave, and as a matter of fact, I had. As usual, I doubted myself and went back.

Vaughn was always saying something critical like, "You aren't putting effort into us," or "I only see you once every other week, "or "we only see each other once every other week," or asking, "how can you go a whole day without speaking to me?" Things like that.

He'd post pictures of us together on Facebook, and I'd make him take them down. He was not happy about a lot of things that made me who I was. It seemed he didn't like me being in control, but I didn't see him as controlling.

It didn't make sense, but I couldn't shake the feeling that something just wasn't right.

I'd asked him on multiple occasions to let me know his secret sin. He swore he didn't have any. I knew it was in there and I was going to find out.

Christmas came around, and Vaughn took me shopping for an outfit to wear to my family's gathering. This was the first time I'd ever brought a guy to our Christmas bash since Deondre years ago. We actually had a wonderful time. Our family gatherings were the place to be.

Vaughn started filming the kids while we were there and even posted the videos to his Facebook page. He was so popular that he had two Facebook pages, one had reached its friendship max, and the other one was closed.

He was still friends with a few of his exes. I saw that as a good sign. I figured, obviously he hadn't done anything too bad to them, or they wouldn't continue to be connected to him, right? I also noticed how his followers seemed to adore him. So, I thought maybe there's something to this guy. I'll hold on to him just in case he's someone special.

We got into it about him filming the kids though.

I told him, "You can't just go around filming people's kids and posting videos."

He was not happy about that and turned on me.

He said, "The only person who has a problem with it is my *so-called* lady." Then he asks, "Was your son there at the party?"

"Yeah," I said.

"You didn't introduce us?"

"No."

"Whoa," he says, "I just don't know what's going on. I mean I thought God had shown me my future wife, but maybe I was wrong."

I'm not sure if that's how we ended again, but we did end it. And like always, I worked hard to get him back. My favorite game, get your man back.

We kept in touch, and I remember one day we were on the subject of women and their smells.

"Your lady smells," he said and did it in such a way that it seemed like a bitch who had been waiting to tell you some news she had on you.

"When?!" I asked. I was heated.

"What if I said every time?"

"Then I'd say you're a liar. I have an ex that I know for a fact would have told me."

I'm calculating in my head how long it's been since I was with Deondre. I also had a *maintenance man* the prior year and he said I tasted like I ate salads every day.

"You don't douche?!"

"No," I said offended, "that's unhealthy."

"It is not," he replies like he has a lady of his own. "It kills bacteria that make you smell."

He's arguing with me like a pure bitch. I get off the phone and think about calling Deondre. I decide not to, remembering why I don't talk to him.

I'm up thinking and thinking. I schedule a doctor's appointment. It confirms a yeast infection. I also had not been doing my usual upkeep.

Even with my *maintenance man* I had been watching my diet and always did lady checks and such. It was becoming clearer to me that I *really* didn't consider *this* man to be *my* man. *So why not leave?*

I did make it my business to tell him I knew what the problem was. It did make me think though, when I started dating him, I felt like I was out of *his* league. So how is it that he was now treating me like *he* was doing *me* a favor.

I put it in his file as *suspect*.

When I saw him, he confirmed that I'd handled the problem.

"You know when a woman has a smell, it's a medical problem," I began. "And I think it's her man's job to inform her, so she can fix it. It was the way you delivered it, ALL WRONG."

He glitched.

His eyes changed, and he became a different person as he argued with me like a bitch, *again*.

"I keep things real," he said. "You just need to learn how to accept the truth. It's a simple matter of washing and douching."

"Douching is equivalent to a person who brushes their teeth and uses mouthwash every day," I said. "It's a cover up for an underlying condition. After the mouthwash wears off their breath will still smell horrible."

He got quiet. I knew I'd stung him. His breath smelt like the morgue's dumpster juice. He was always using mouthwash. I could tell he was surprised I snapped back at him.

I remember telling my mom the things I was doing to get him back. She was exasperated. "Just leave him alone," she said. "You only want him back so you can discard him like an old toy."

"No, I don't think so. Not this time, I don't think.," I said but wondering if she had a point. *Why did I want him back?* Part of me wanted to find out if he was real or not. The other part was thinking, "And if he is, I'd like to cash in my winnings."

In the meantime, Desmond had come to visit me at work one day. As I was walking him out, he put one hand on the wall on either side of me to block me in.

"Desmond, I told you I'm trying to settle down."

"People like you and I don't change," he said. "It's impossible. He doesn't have to know."

"Says the man who got married."

"Yeah! And look at me. You'll be the same way."

"He won't know, but I'll know. You know the single me not the booed up me. When I'm with someone, I give 100% that way it can never be said it was my fault."

"Does he know you're different? Have you told him?"

"No, there's no reason to tell him anything. Look, you have to go. If you can't behave and keep your hands to yourself, then you can't come back."

"Alright," he says. "I'll be here whenever you're ready."

Valentine's day came, and Vaughn took me out, but there were no gifts. I was highly disappointed. He also took me to the Cheesecake Factory after I'd told him once before that to me the Cheesecake Factory was the new McDonalds for dates.

This time I was in no mood to be coy and drop hints that I was *not* impressed. I showed it on my face too.

In March he took me out for my birthday, and I want to say it was the Cheesecake Factory *again*. I was beginning to think he was doing this on purpose. On the surface we looked so happy; we pretended so well. We were so passive aggressive with each other.

Sometimes he was just straight out aggressive.

I remember I was staying over with him once and I wanted to watch something on TV. I was telling him what I wanted to watch, and he just snapped.

He said, "Not everything is always all about you," and took the remote. I was just looking like, *who is this guy*?

Any other time he was THE sweetest guy ever.

Whenever he would glitch, I would put it in his file as *suspect*. Men didn't snap at me. The only one who ever had in that manner was Anton. I didn't peg Vaughn as being abusive, so what was he?

Time went on, and I finally introduced my son to Vaughn. Elijah absolutely loved hanging with Vaughn. My son was always worried about how lonely I was and wanted me to get married. So yeah, he was happy.

One evening Vaughn called. "Why haven't we spoken all day?"

"Well you know I get so busy," I say, "the day just flies by."

"Busy doing what," Vaughn asks sounding unconvinced.

"Well you do know I'm a wonderful full-time mom, I run my own business. I'm trying to go back to school," I said, confident that I'd just shut that down.

"I happen to know that at the most, on your busiest day, you work five hours max."

Note to self, stop talking so much.

Vaughn went on to lecture me about how when two people love each other they don't go all day without speaking. "I never, never get tired of you," he says.

He was really upset when I up and decided I wanted a job for the summer.

"No, don't get a job. It will cut into our time. If you do get one, do Uber or something flexible. How about I work more hours and help you with the bills?"

"Aw honey, you're so sweet," I swooned. "You already have so much to do. That wedding venue we looked at is expensive. You know I don't have much money for the wedding. You still have to buy me that promise ring and engagement ring. I can at the very least pay my own bills."

I was actually trying to put even more space between us until I could figure out what exactly was going on. I remember someone even asked was I going to work to avoid my "boyfriend."

Finally, Vaughn and I head on our first trip together. We head to New York for his uncle's funeral. I met his girls and was I in for a treat. They told me to run. And boy did I believe them. We got back to the hotel after the funeral, and I told him to go on in and that I'd be right behind him. He says, "Since when do we separate?"

I wanted to call my mom so bad. Vaughn wouldn't leave me alone, so we head up together. I told him what the girls said, and he was furious and hurt. He cried and gave me a sob story and called his mom in front of me and again I filed it under *suspect* but stayed with him.

Another trip comes around and another and another. We were going to weddings, birthday parties, and whatever occasion came up. He sensed a different me and said, "You know I never knew you liked trips so much."

I said, "They're my favorite."

So, he started planning a trip to Boca Raton for us that following August. He'd gotten plane tickets and took care of almost everything right down to new expensive shoes for me. He'd told me what to pack and told me to get his queen and her king shirts made by my brother's company.

I thought it was whack and my brother picked on me about it, but oh well.

"This is as close as you've ever been to marrying someone," my brother teased.

"No," I said, "I've been closer."

"I mean on your end," he laughed, "as a willing participant."

I laughed too and said, "Well I'm getting older and broker, so I've got to nail down some security."

I was excited. I'd never gone anywhere without my family. I tended to stay close to them because they considered me "special."

I was shopping to head out of town and my cousin Tonya called me and left a message for me to call her back.

I called her back.

"I just wanted you to know that Steven and I are really close. We both serve on the youth committee at church," she begins. "He has asked me to be a mother figure to his child."

"Well," I said. "Who am I to stand in ya'lls way if you're getting what you need from each other."

"What could I need from him?" She asked.

"Obviously something," I said, and we ended the conversation.

A day or two later Vaughn and I fly out.

Again, I'm *acting* happy, but I'm *really* wishing I was with someone, anyone else. Much like one of our dates we stayed at the Renaissance. Beautiful hotel. But I didn't want to be there with him.

When we pulled up, and I saw where we were going, I said, "Oh you're going to love it here, they have TVs in the mirrors."

I used every chance I could to deflate his balloon. He was always acting as if he was so much more high class than I was because I wasn't high maintenance. He used to say stuff like, "A woman should wake up in the morning and sneak out of bed and get fully made up and then get back in bed, so she's beautiful when her husband wakes up."

He'd even asked me once how I ever became spoiled as if to say I wasn't even that pretty to have guys spoil me the way I think I should. He would also tell me how good of a guy he was and bring up how good to me he was as if to say I should be lucky and treat him better.

My response to him was that every man was good to me. "You can't even get my number," I said, "unless I *think* you're a gentleman. I'm not looking for a *good* man; I know plenty. What I'm waiting for is *my* man, the one God has for me. So that's what I'm trying to find out. Not if you're good but are you mine."

That particular night he took me to look at wedding rings. I guess I was supposed to be excited. He ushered me through that night like something straight out of a movie. I should have been excited if he were someone else. Most nights like this I thought, "If only this were Bruce."

On that same trip, I pulled out lingerie that night and waited for him to come out of the bathroom. He just kind of looked at me like, "well, I guess we're doing this."

I put it in the folder as *suspect.*

He was always telling me I acted as if sex was a chore and I never initiated, so I was trying to initiate.

This was the very reason I wouldn't; this nigga didn't like pussy.

So, what does he like?

I'd even told him once that I didn't think he desired me. I knew what it was like to be desired by a man, and he didn't. He apologized for it, but again, it was in the file.

On the trip, gay guys came around us at the airport and sat by us on the plane, and I watched Vaughn the whole time.

I pretended to look at him *lovingly* or like I was trying to catch his attention, but I was waiting to see if he was checking the guys out. He didn't though. He sat very still and stiff, almost uncomfortable looking straight ahead.

Fucking *suspect* file.

The trip came to a bitter end.

We argued about me eating at the airport. I didn't want food; I wanted chips. He went on this long tantrum about how I don't need chips and its unhealthy, blah, blah. I knew then it would be over soon. I couldn't go through this.

He bought me a 3-piece meal from Bojangles. Talk about unhealthy. We missed our flight ignoring each other and once finally home it was just awkward. I decided to go ahead and smoothed things over as we had a trip with Elijah coming up.

CONFESSION TEN:

God's Tests

> *"If anyone ever touches my son, I'll kill everyone involved: me, him and the perp."*

Vaughn once told me about a friend of his that had "accidentally" sent dick pics to his daughter. She was grown; however, the daughter had accused him of *suspicious* stuff before when she was younger.

Vaughn agreed the guy was wrong, he was trying to convince me that the guy needed to be forgiven and loved anyway. Yada, yadda.

It rubbed me very wrong.

We talked the *entire* way to the amusement park about how I hated pedophiles. He agreed that he did too, but you could cut the tension with a knife.

I was worked up.

I said, "If anyone *ever* touches my son, I'll kill everyone involved: me, him and the perp."

He said, "You're sick, you need to talk to someone about that."

I said, "No, sick people just need to stay away from me and mine."

We head into the park, and things were just weird. The vibe was off. We all got on the scary house ride, and I ride with my arm across Elijah so that I can feel any movement should it happen in the dark.

We leave the park with an awkward ride home.

I prayed, "God things are going in a direction I'm not too sure about. I need answers, talk to me."

The next day, I went to church and got in line for prayer. When I tell you my Bishop has always been the truth; she laid hands on me, and I cried and cried. She hugged me, told me she loved me and that it would be ok. She usually told me things, but not that day.

I can't remember what night it was, but soon after that, the revelations hit me like a ton of bricks. My son Elijah had only been around Vaughn a handful of times, but like a slideshow, God replayed everything in the file back to me.

#HeTriedIt: *Remember that day at the restaurant he was standing directly behind Elijah? Why?*

#HeTriedIt: *Remember the day he asked Elijah had he been daydreaming about him? You said, "Dudes don't daydream about each other." He tried to normalize it and said, "You know what I mean, like think about me and what I'm doing when I'm not with you guys."*

#HeTriedIt: *Remember you always felt he didn't desire you?*

#HeTriedIt: *Remember in the grocery store he again stood directly behind Elijah, almost penis to butt, as Elijah was leaning on the grocery cart?*

#HeTriedIt: *Remember when he stayed at your house and tried to sleep in the living room in the middle of the night* *blaming it on allergies and you had to make him get up and get locked back in your room?*

#HeTriedIt: *Remember his Facebook post condemning Preacher Jamal Bryant on the Preacher's TV show for a comment, but he posted footage of Eddie Long's forgiveness snippet and said how we needed to love and support him as Christians and not condemn him?*

I guess cheating on your spouse is a worse crime than taking advantage of little kids.

#HeTriedIt: *Remember how you would cringe every time he tickled Elijah? Elijah is beyond tickling age.*

#HeTriedIt: *In New York, he introduced you to his girls only, not his boys. Why?!*

#HeTriedIt: *Remember he asked you when you were gonna let Elijah go to the men's bathroom by himself and learn what men do. "Are you going to let him grow pubic hair and still have him using the women's restroom," he said. Why is Elijah all of a sudden so mature he should go to the men's room alone but still young enough to be tickled?*

#HeTriedIt: *He's been pretending he wants to marry you, but there still is no ring.*

#HeTriedIt: *Remember he tried to move in with you a few months ago offering to pay you exactly $591 a month for rent? What man buys you a $500 handbag, $100 shoes, encourages you against getting a summer job by offering to help with your bills, yet can't afford to pay your mortgage or buy himself a car by now?*

#HeTriedIt: *He's after your son*

Vaughn had tried it. He had attempted to make a move on MY son! When I tell you, I was sick to my stomach for days...

I began short texting him; I didn't know how I wanted to handle it. After about two weeks I started talking to him again. I explained that I wasn't well and that God had told me his secret.

He still insisted that there was no secret.

I started posting on Facebook, a lot of facts about pedophiles. Every time we talked he wouldn't bring it up even though I was sure he'd seen the posts.

One morning I said, "I heard your song and thought about you, no condemnation."

He got a little snippy and said, "When you give your life to Christ, God looks down and sees the blood, not your wrong. No condemnation."

Another day when I was telling him about his secret, he said, "I don't know what you're talking about. What sin is it."

I said, "I won't say, I want you to tell me."

He said, "This secret sin I *supposedly* have, what triggered you to think this?"

In my mind, I said, "There's no way in hell I'm about to make things difficult for the next woman by revealing to you what tipped me off." But instead, I said, "Nothing triggered anything, God told me."

We kept at it for as long as we could. Each of us trying to make the other believe that we were a couple. I was being *really* nice to him and he picked up on it and ran. He wouldn't fall for it this time. He said, "Why are you being so sweet to me; this isn't you."

He was right.

Eventually, we stopped talking altogether. I tried to get my son's father to send some goons after him but to no avail. I'd prepared things around the house hoping he'd be crazy enough to come by. I fantasized over and over about tying him up with zip ties and making him my pet:

I would move Elijah to a family member's house temporarily. I would keep Vaughn in my tub. I would visit him every day and think of new ways to torture him.

Besides, I needed an example. I talked a lot of shit, and I figured I now had the opportunity to turn into a *real* monster. I had to show people I was every bit as crazy as I say I am.

Excitement turned to fear as I went through what I can only describe as PTSD. I was jolted awake at night with my heart racing at the thought of someone being in my house. I'd look out into the dark house and see a shadowy figure.

I preferred to keep the house pitch black. Vaughn once tried to keep a light on the way he did at his own home.

"Why do you keep it so dark?"

"If someone breaks in they have to fumble around before finding a switch," I said. "But me, I know my house. In those few minutes, while they're fumbling, I can put my plan into action."

Since I had always imagined horror scenarios as a girl, I didn't have any trouble devising a plan.

One day, I'm angry and fussing at God again.

"God! I'm furious," I say. "Why do you keep testing me in the area of my child? Satan I'm mad at you too, but I know you can't do anything without God allowing it. You all owe me. You all owe me big. I tell you what? For putting me through that bullshit, I need one of you to bring back one of two people."

I knew I really wanted Bruce back but would take either one.

I said, "First come, first served. You want a show? Bring one of them back and I'll give you a show."

You should really be careful what you ask for.

CHAPTER TEN: A SCARY MOVIE
Get Out!

One day while I was taking care of some emails, I glanced down at google chat. It no longer said *denied* over Bruce's face.

What?!

I hover over it just to be sure. Usually when I hover over his avatar a red crossed out circle would appear. This time his avatar stayed intact. That freaked me out. I should have been used to things like that, but I was in disbelief and actually scared.

Who brought him back, God or Satan?

I decided what the hell and reached out to him.

"Hey, I need to talk to you," I said cautiously.

It wasn't long before he replied, "Do you want me to call you, are we talking in person or what?"

I told him to call.

We talked and soon began talking regularly. I told him about Vaughn who we now called Pedo. I told him about how scared I was. Somehow, he brought moving back in with me up, and within a few months he was back.

I wish I could tell you we moved in together, fell in love and lived happily ever after. But by now, I think you see the pattern my life takes. I trusted him as much as I could, which really wasn't much at all. Sometimes I wondered if he somehow knew Pedo and they had a plan together.

One day he brought up wishing he could do work helping with sex trafficking. Even if it was nothing but tracking and information, a reporting and locating type thing.

"You won't even help me find information out on Pedo," I snapped. "What do you mean?!"

"Man! You're obsessed with him," he snapped back. "Let it go! You want to stop thinking about him then you have to move on. I'd swear you're in love with him."

"Who said I *wanted* to stop thinking about him?

I never said that. I *want* to think about him every day of his life until I find out he's gotten what he deserves."

"You're psycho!"

"Why do you always say that like you're surprised?" I said now visibly frustrated. "I was honest with you from the start. You know I have issues. You keep staying so what does that say about you?"

"You're right," he says with recognition. "Something's wrong with my dumbass too."

"We should start our own business looking for these people. You know I've always wanted to kill somebody," I whispered. "At least they'd deserve it."

He looks at me like, *yeah right.*

Bruce was one of those people who doubted I was as crazy as I tried to convince people I was. He was the same way though. He was always saying that he was going to kill someone for one reason or another. I told him many times that I should be scared of him, but I wasn't.

Bruce and I weren't in a relationship; we were really just roommates. However, a few days after he found out that I was dating someone and that it was getting serious, he stopped talking to me for like a month and a half.

Finally, I'd had enough of the silent treatment. I missed him.

I passed through his room and tried to get on his bed. He blocked me.

"Morgan!? Do you want to die today?!"

"I just want to talk," I pleaded.

"Do not jump on top of me," he threatened. "I promise you I'm going to choke the shit out of you."

I hopped right on top of him and rolled to the other side of his bed. He jumped on the bed, rolled to his side and grabbed my trachea.

"Get out!"

"I'm trying," I screeched.

"Your feet aren't on the floor."

"I can't reach it," I cried.

I got to be honest; I was a little scared. I was always pushing him to his limits, and I knew that in some way he was sick too. On the other hand, I was a bit excited too.

He finally let go. I laid down and got comfortable.

"No! Get out!"

"Well, first of all, I got to know," I said totally calm now. "What technique is that you were using? I've been choked several times, and no one has ever grabbed me by the trachea."

"It's easier to kill someone by just quickly snapping their trachea," he explained. "When you grabbed them by the neck you have to exert a lot of energy and wait a long time."

He was such a nerd and so sexy with all of that knowledge. I smiled to myself in the dark.

"What's been going on with you," I ask.

He started to complain about something at work.

"Oh, I'm sorry," I said sarcastically. "Is *that* why you've had an attitude with me?"

"No!" He shouted and got quiet as if he almost didn't mean to answer so quickly.

"Well why haven't you been talking to me and you were so mean to me before that?"

"Because I hate you and I want to kill you, now get out."

"I haven't even bothered you for the last month and a half."

"So just because you give me a few weeks break I'm supposed to forget I hate you? Why are you still in here?!"

"Well, I'm only trying to make us both happy," I laugh. "You want to kill me, and I've always wanted to be in a scary movie."

He didn't laugh. I continued to lay there. Eventually, I began to get comfortable and relax. Ten minutes more goes by, and he must have sensed I would fall asleep soon.

"Get Out!" He screamed.

Needless to say, my hopes for being in a scary movie weren't going to happen this day.

CONFESSION ELEVEN:
The 'What Ifs'

"I was sneaky too,
but at least I was good at it."

"Yes, you did," Bruce my roommate blurted out. "You've imagined the worse ever since Elijah was born."

As much as I hated to admit it, Bruce was right. I had imagined every horrible *what if* imaginable happening to my child.

One time I'd messed up my schedule and wasn't able to go on a field trip with Elijah. He was worried I wouldn't let him go. As much as I didn't want him to go without me, I knew I had to let him go. I rushed and got him a cell phone at the last minute to carry with him, just in case, and so I could track him.

As I dropped him off at school that morning, he looked at me and giggled.

"What?" I asked.

"Your face," he giggled more.

He knew I was about to cry.

Sure enough, as soon as the bus drove off, I cried like a baby. I just knew *this* was the day, the day something horrible would happen to my baby. I went home and got back in the bed. I blasted *Suicide Squad* through my earbuds and cried myself to sleep. Every time I'd wake up I'd cry and then pray myself back to sleep. This went on until finally, I *had* to get up to make my 4:30 appointment.

After my client, I went to Elijah's school and waited for his bus to arrive. I anxiously waited for him to step off the bus. Once I saw his face, instant relief.

My mental illness and my love for my son made life extra hard on us both. I smothered him, and I knew he didn't like it nor was it healthy. I had on many occasions thought, "God, just take him back."

Bruce frequently called us Norma and Norman Bates.

You see, there were things others noticed, but my roommate was the only one big and bad enough to call me on it, straight on. He wouldn't let me *BS* my way around it.

"We need to have a serious talk," he'd say. "Something's wrong with your son. Either you're oblivious to it, or you know, and you're negligent. Either way, you need to get him help and raise him right or give him up to someone who's going to do the job. You spoil him, and you never discipline him. What do you think is going to happen when he's a grown man, and a woman tells him no, and he's never heard it before?"

I was furious!

He could have left out the *give him up* part. NEVER! NEVER!

Bruce was right though. We were Norma and Norman Bates.

Bruce and I went back and forth.

"Your son has a blank look in his eyes, and he likes violence a *little* too much for someone his age," Bruce continued.

"Yeah," I said defensively. "Well, I did too, but I'm fine."

"Stop fucking comparing yourself to your son!"

Again, he was right, and I knew it. I hovered over my son not only to protect *him* but to protect *others* from him.

Elijah had always been *different.* He was the sweetest, most perfect kid I knew. Then again, so was I. My son's patterns looked a lot like mine. This scared me because I always felt had I been born a dude I'd be dangerous. Now I wondered if my son would be the danger I had feared I'd be.

I called his dad.

"It's time we come out of denial," I said trying not to freak out. "We can't keep turning a blind eye to what Elijah does. He's getting too old."

"What do you mean?"

"I think he's a low-key bully," I confessed. "We can't keep calling the school saying, 'Someone's messing with our kid and keep that kid away from our son.' It's not everyone else every time. The teacher even says he's sneaky and he's messing with the kids."

"Messing with kids. How? What is he doing to them?"

"I don't know," I said quickly becoming irritated with him for pretending to be ignorant to what we both knew. "But when she said sneaky, I believed her. He does *try* to be. I was sneaky too, but at least I was good at it. Elijah isn't."

"I'm glad you finally admitted you were sneaky," he said. "I knew when I met you; you looked sneaky."

"Whatever. Shut up. I'm being serious," I said growing frustrated. "I've seen it with my own eyes, and I just let it go."

"Yeah, something happened that I never told you about because I didn't want you to worry. One weekend when he was at my Mom's, I had to threaten him real bad. I told him I was going to come discipline him. Mama said Jay kept bothering Elijah and then all of a sudden, they heard screaming and hollering coming from Elijah's bedroom. They all went back to his room, and Elijah had Jay's leg locked and wouldn't let go. When he finally let go, they said Jay just slid around the floor for the rest of the day. He couldn't stand up on the leg. They thought they were going to have to take him to the hospital."

Silence.

Then, I'm not sure who started first but one of us snickered, and we both giggled uncontrollably for a minute.

"It's really not funny though," I said sobering up. "Think about it, he's your child, and he's mine. You're violent to the extreme when someone does something to you. I'm violent simply because I like to see people hurting; it gives me joy."

"Now you're starting to scare me a little bit."

"I'm scared too, that's what I'm telling you. I want Elijah to know how to protect himself since he's tiny, but I don't want him hurting people. I've been looking for a counselor to take him to. I really want the one he used to go to, but that's a $100 a pop. That's why it'd be helpful if his daddy could get back to doing his part."

"I know, I know," he said. "I'm trying, soon you won't have to worry about anything."

"Something else I didn't tell you," I sighed. "You remember what happened between Elijah and Kaleigh right? Well, the counselor said Elijah got upset and confessed that he was the abuser in that situation. She asked me if it could be possible, I told her I didn't think so but -"

"No, no, no that's enough," he said shaking his head. "I can't hear anymore. Just look into the counseling, we'll do what we have to do."

Long story short, I believed my baby was not exactly well either.

CHAPTER ELEVEN: GIRL IN PEARLS

A Fetish

I met Cassie when I worked at my pet job. Even though I quit, she and I stayed in touch. Well, she kept in touch with me. She didn't have many friends and she didn't drive either. I guess she felt we were friends because she would always confide in me about her problems.

Cassie was one of those black chicks who desperately wanted to be white. The platinum wigs, fake valley-girl accent, and incessant chatter about nothing were nearly more than I could take.

One night she decides she wants to hang out and go to a fetish party. I couldn't go but told her the next time I was free, we could check it out or something.

She attempted to warn me about *those* types of parties. I laughed inside. She had no idea.

"Don't be shocked Morgan," Cassie says. "At these things, people are naked and doing things you may not be used to."

"I think I'll be ok," I said calmly. "I'm not easily shocked."

I finally get some free time and invite her out to go dancing. We head out and strike up a conversation.

"So how did your date go last night?"

"Depends on how in depth I can get," she says coyly.

"You're fine," I say already bored. "Whatever."

She starts to talk about how she got fucked for four hours straight, and she's all bruised and sore.

I got the feeling she was trying to shock me. I wasn't impressed. Unlike Cassie, I don't care to share the details of my personal life with everyone I meet.

"First date action, hunh?" I say just to keep the conversation going.

"Second date," Cassie corrects me.

I don't know what difference that made, but I let her think it did. I generally made a man wait about two months or so.

Cassie goes on to reveal that her date was a 46-year-old white man.

"Oh, ok," I say, still not interested.

Looking back, I remember thinking that Cassie was acting a bit weird, trying too hard or something to impress me, but I didn't think much of it at the time.

"Yeah, I only date white guys," she continues, "like the kind of men you date."

My antenna goes up, but I let that comment ride. We get to the first bar, and this guy approaches us. He is clearly interested in me and we begin to make small talk. Then he offers to buy us all drinks. Cassie gets excited at the wad of cash he pulls out to pay with and nudges me.

After being there for a while, we decide it was time to head to the next bar. We ride with him, and once inside, Cassie remembers she left her phone in his car. Max hands her his keys so he and I can keep talking, but Cassie comes up with some bogus excuse about being bad at remembering where we parked.

So, Max agrees to walk her to the car. They come back shortly and, in my opinion, she's making *guilt faces* as she tugs her skirt hem down.

I'm wondering, *did they do something while they were at the car?*

Looking back, she could've just been pretending to be ashamed at how short her skirt hem was and pulling it down fishing for a compliment.

I tried to put that shit in the *suspect* file, and keep it moving. I mean just because he was pushing up on me, didn't make him mine. But it was disrespectful.

We get to the next bar and order more drinks. I considered offering to pay for the drinks. I didn't want Max thinking we were using him for a ride and his cash. Who knows he could have boyfriend potential.

Then something odd happens.

I find myself seething about what *may* have happened at the car. My jealousy over him surprises me. I lean over to smell Max's face, and he tries to kiss me.

"I'm trying to smell you, not kiss you," I told him.

"Oh ok," he chuckles, clearly embarrassed. "I'm going to the bathroom."

When he comes back, we head down to another bar.

Cassie grabs his arm saying she's about to fall and needs his assistance. They walk off ahead of me, and I'm like, *what the fuck is going on*?

After what seems like too long he finally figures out something wasn't right and comes back to get me. I was so close to saying, *let's go* and not talk to either of them ever again, but I decided to handle it a different way.

We get to the club, and before walking in, I ask, "Do we have rules?"

"That depends?" Max asks, now clearly confused, "what you got planncd?"

"No plans, just asking before we get in here. I don't want to be *disrespectful*." I say and look directly at Cassie.

Then I look at Max. I'm feeling him out. His face looks concerned, so I lighted up a bit. Maybe he's clueless to what Cassie's doing. Men can be stupid too.

We head in.

There are some white people there, lots of black people, but it's a good mix. Max finds a lounger across from the big screen TV where a game was on. There were also three white girls across from him.

Cassie wants to go dance. I tell her to go ahead, and she insists that I come. I tell Max that I'll be back.

We go, and she starts to dance with a group. Most of the crowd is young, so I head back to Max. She notices I'm missing and heads back too. She begs me to come out again. So, I do. This time she leaves me.

I'm looking all around, and when I head back to Max, that's where I find her. She sees me coming and asks, "Where did you go?"

"I was right there the whole time," I told her.

"This guy tried to kidnap me," she pouted, "and I came to Max for help, and he wouldn't even help me."

"What did you expect him to do," I asked.

Max chimes in, "You're grown. If you want to leave with some guy, I can't stop you."

Eventually, she suggests that we go to the bar and order some drinks. While I'm waiting, she goes missing again. I circle back and there she is sitting with Max, talking.

They talk a bit longer, and again she wants to go dance.

I'm walking towards the dance floor and slow down to check if she's behind me and she is not. There's a divider between where Max was and where I was. I decide to wait at the corner where I could see him just to see if she shows back up there.

Sure enough, she does.

She bends down and whispers something in his ear, he starts to look around and spots me. He points to me and says, "There she is."

Having been spotted, I head back over.

"Where'd you go," she excitedly shouts.

"No, where did *you* go" I ask her. "We literally walked 3 feet, and you went missing."

Then I asked Max, "Am I interrupting something here?"

"I'm just sitting here," he responds looking as puzzled as I was. "I don't know what *she's* doing."

I calmed down some, realizing I was drunk and could be overly sensitive.

"Is it me," I asked. "or is *she* acting weird?"

"Maybe she's just young like you said. I don't know, but maybe next time we can try this again without her."

I felt better.

We head to the dance floor again.

This time a guy wants to dance with me. Here it is I think to myself, payback. I wasn't disrespectful with it though. I kept it classy, basically doing the two-step.

The guy was hitting me with some of his best lines. We were speaking back and forth in each other's ears over the music.

"You're not from around here are you?" He asks. "You look like the CEO of something."

"What," I laugh. "Why do you think that?"

"You look important, like a boss."

"I'm old and dressed like a lady. That's what you see."

He said, "You *are* aren't you?"

"A very small one," I reply as I laugh.

Bodak Yellow comes on, and I begin to sway with more effort.

"This song makes me feel hard," I told him.

"You're wearing pearls," he says sarcastically. "Unless you're a Mafia Donna, I'm not sure how hard you can be in pearls."

I laugh, and he put his arm around my waist. The song ends, and I go sit with Max. Cassie gets up and goes to dance with the guy I was just with.

Now it's all making sense. The chick has issues.

She motions for me to come back out to the dance floor and I do. She *then* motions for Max. Just to be clear, I hold my hand out to receive him, so they don't get any ideas. The song ends, and the four of us head to the couch. Max sits as I stand in front of him. He's been holding my clutch with my flats, and I reach for them. He reaches down and assists me in removing my heels and sliding on my flats. I sit beside him as a dude from the dance floor gives me the *'really'* face from the other side of Cassie. I shrug, he shakes his head and sits back.

Cassie whispers, "Save me," in my ear.

I look over, and dude is now sleeping. Like hard. I'm like, "Save you from what?"

Max thinks it's hilarious. He's like, "Yeah. He has no game." He seems relieved that there was no real threat.

The club shuts down, and we head out. We're walking back to the car, and Cassie says, "Hey Morgan, do you know this guy?" She points to this tall, dark, and very handsome guy. "He says he went to school with you."

"Oh hey," I squeal as I go up to hug him. I don't really remember him, but I'm only trying to turn the knife a little.

Max clears his throat as if to say, "Woman stop all of that squealing. I'm standing *right* here you know."

I smile, satisfied that he has *now* felt the sting.

We drop Cassie off, then he drives me to my car. I agree to follow him to his house for one more drink.

He's still talking about how whack the guy was and how I talked to him for like 20 minutes on the dance floor. We were in his kitchen, and he insisted that I do a breathalyzer.

"You need to sober up before you drive home," he says. "I'd hate for something to happen to you."

"Really," I say and then to test the waters. "I thought guys like drunk girls."

"Not me," he says. "I want you to remember everything that happens."

I have to admit that line was impressive.

"I was jealous though back at the club," he admits. Then he tries to ram his tongue down my throat.

That was enough for me. Turns out he was more of Cassie's type after all.

I push him back.

"I've been thinking about bending you over a table all night long," he says.

I thought about it, for all of a second. Like I told Cassie, I make them wait.

On my way home, I thought about Cassie and how she broke the girl code. I don't hang out with females who think we have to compete.

I don't know but it felt like she only wanted Max because he seemed to want me. That was foul to me.

Clearly, *she thought* since I was in pearls that I wasn't the type of chick to bash her head in over being disrespected.

I let it ride.

But it was added to the list of things I would have to get off my chest one day.

CONFESSION TWELVE:
Between Good and Evil

"I wonder if God is punishing me..."

This person had been contacting me on my business line asking if I had an appointment for the same day and time, each time they called. I thought it was weird that this person wanted a *specific* day and time and although that day and time hadn't been available, they never asked to make a future appointment.

But people were weird like that, so I let it go, until now.

They were messaging me again.

This time I responded that I could, in fact, take them that evening. I instructed them to print the online intake form and bring it with them if possible. They immediately informed me that they were a regular client, but it had been a while since their last visit.

I didn't have a clue, but I was eager to find out.

As soon as he walked in, I began to remember who he was. Malcolm was the kind of man you didn't forget.

"Go on back and get comfortable," I said. "I will be in momentarily."

As I stood in the hallway, I'm literally about to explode.

How dare you, I thought. *I just experienced a personal tragedy, and you come in here wanting me to do whatever.*

I calm down enough and decide to go inside where he's waiting.

It's easy money, I thought.

"So, I do remember you," I said.

"Is that right?" he says.

"Yeah."

"Is it ok I'm here?"

"Yeah," I say hiding my irritation. "It's fine. What can I do for you today?"

"Just rub me here," he says brushing his fingers across his broad chest and lightly resting on his nipples, "on top of the sheet."

I begin to rub his nipples, and he begins to talk to me about all sorts of sexual things. Somethings I am into, but others I say, "For the sake of your fantasy I could say that I'm into that, but honestly I'm not (eating pussy for example). But hey if that's what you're into, I can arrange a show for you." I say.

"Is your friend a prostitute?" He asks quietly.

"No, just a girl that likes to have a good time."

"Can we take this session past an hour?" He asks.

"No," I say. Noting that we had about 15 minutes left.

"Do you have AIDS?"

"It wouldn't be safe to answer that either way," I say matter-of-factly. "It doesn't matter anyway considering we haven't done anything."

"Since you won't answer the question, it must mean that you do and now I must have it too."

"I wouldn't tell you I'm clean and run the risk of you raping me."

"I promise that's not something I'd ever do."

"Well, clearly you don't trust me, and I don't trust you," I say. "I think it's best we keep it that way."

Then he starts to tear up and a single tear escapes and slides down his smooth dark skin.

"Ok, so I think I know what's going on here," I say in my clinical professional voice. "You feel extreme guilt for cheating on your wife, and so you're sure that you'll be punished by getting AIDS?"

He nods his freshly cut head yes.

"I do not have AIDS," I say. "Even if I did, *we* haven't done anything. I advise you to talk to your wife about your needs. Maybe get counseling and let her know how serious and normal your needs are before you *actually* cheat and *actually* run the real risk of contracting AIDS by committing adultery."

He doesn't say anything.

Being dirty, I ask, "Do you think she'd let a woman come in and open her up?"

"No," he says, "not at all." Then he focuses on me. "It looked as if *you* were going to cry just then."

"No," I said as I quietly sat beside him.

He lay there looking up at the ceiling as I looked at him.

"Well," he persisted, "you looked sad at least."

"Well, I've got things going on," I admitted.

"So, you *do* have AIDS?"

"No," I sighed heavily. "I don't. I lost someone I love."

I briefly told him the details, but only a few.

"I wonder if God is punishing me because I have desires like this, to do what we are doing and what we've talked about doing," I confessed. "I used to have a phobia of catching AIDS too, so I know what you're feeling. But then my son came along, and *he* became my obsession. So much so that I no longer was concerned about AIDS as much."

He sat up still naked and swung his legs over the bed and said, "Let's pray."

We ended our time with me saying, "Maybe God had us come together for closure, and now maybe we can find it together."

"From now on," he says, "when I text you, just say no."

I agreed.

He paid me.

We hugged, and he left.

CHAPTER TWELVE: THE BIG PAYBACK
It's All About Them

After the last couple of years I'd had, I was looking for someone who was going to pay for all of the shit I'd gone through.

I'd gotten back in touch with Monica. She was DEFINITELY a possibility for my revenge.

I decided to text Desmond:

Des?

I texted him, but it wasn't until the next day that he replied.

Yes, it's Desmond.
Sorry, I fell asleep early.
How are you?

Finally, I thought. I hurriedly responded:

I'm good.

He then sent:

Can you talk?

I could feel the tension leaving me already, and I responded:

Yes

The phone rings.

"What's going on?" Desmond shouted in the phone.

"Not much," I say. "I need to get out."

"You know my life is so boring without you. When I hear from you, it's like Christmas. Let's try to get together this weekend."

"Ok, I'm going to try to line something up." I said, and I swear I could hear the wheels turning in his head immediately.

"Ok, it's fine if we line something up, but I need to see *you*," Desmond said suddenly timid. "I know you hate when I ask but..."

"What?" I was confused. "No, I don't, what are you talking about?"

"You. I need you, just you." Then he was silent.

"Oh...," I said with realization.

"See, *that*, **that's** what I'm talking about," Desmond said.

"Yeah...*that*...ok, I'll let you know," I said as we hung up. Desmond was a short, stocky guy. He dressed impeccably, always smelled great, and was very persuasive. I was actually beginning to look forward to the evening.

I decided to go ahead and call Monica. "Honestly, I don't know if she can satisfy my physical urges," I said out loud.

Then I thought of a possibility that would kill two birds with one stone. If I could make it a group event, I could get my payback with Monica *and* be have my urges satisfied by watching her and Desmond.

Hmm, now that's a plan that could work, I thought.

So, I texted Monica:

Hey, I'm free for the weekend. You?

Almost immediately she texts back:

Absolutely

Then I texted Desmond:

You game for the weekend?

It wasn't long before he responded:

Just tell me when and where!

Initially, we were going to go to a neighboring town so Desmond's wife wouldn't catch him out, so we decided to go to a private party. It was at someone's house.

We get there and its mostly white people. They're doing weird *white people* shit. There's a couple lying on the couch across from us. The guy is sitting, and the girl is lying with her head in his lap. Every now and again he'll choke her some. When he's done with that, he rests his hand back between her legs. She's wearing a dress and obviously no panties.

I'm excited and waiting to see how far they will go. Desmond and I nudge each other and gaze lovingly into each other's eyes. This just goes on forever and gets a little boring.

Monica was undressed almost as soon as we entered the house, but now she too was bored and ready to go dancing and drinking.

Desmond decides we should go to a strip club. He's sure his wife won't be there.

We leave the house and head for the strip club and find seats. Desmond sits so that I have to lean over him to look at the dancers over the balcony. I eventually get up to sit on his lap.

"That's what I've been waiting for you to do," he says.

Monica, young and not used to being a lady, hops up and goes to the bar to order a drink.

Being a lady, I wait until the waitress comes and have my drinks ordered for me. One thing I hate about women these days. We want to act *soooo* independent, but it's a cheap cover-up. Sure, I can do everything myself, but I shouldn't have to. Everyone knows I like being treated well. If I have to pay for my own drinks, food, entertainment, etc. I can stay the fuck home and have a grand ole time by myself.

If a guy wants you to come out, leave your child/children, find a sitter, do your hair, etc. then it better be worth it.

Women jump up so fast to please a man that we have them trained to believe that it's all about them.

NO, THE HELL IT IS NOT!

Anyway, my drinks were ordered for me and brought to me. After drinking a bit Desmond whispers, "I think we can *slut* her out."

I really and honestly had not considered doing anything to the girl myself, I just wanted to use the night to pay her back for disrespecting me.

He says, "Look at her, she wants to have a good time." He pulls out some one-dollar-bills and hands them to her. "Go tip one of the girls."

Monica takes the money and heads over to one of the strippers. She tips the girl, engages in a conversation, and a bit of a dance-off. When she comes back, she mentions how horny she is.

"You should do something about that," Desmond says.

"Are you volunteering," She snaps back at him.

The snaps go back and forth a bit, and finally, we decide to leave where they pick back up with the banter.

"Well, I'm sure Morgan isn't going to want to just sit in the car and watch us fuck."

"You don't know what I might want to do," I say fully in control.

At the car, I instruct Desmond to head to an office he and I use for "business."

We get there, and one of my work tables is set up. I lift Monica's dress and slide her panties down. Immediately I smell onions. It's no big deal to me, and I'm sure Desmond doesn't care. I take her tiny panties and stuff them in her mouth. I take her dress off and have her lay down on the table on her back.

I'd asked Desmond to buy me some gloves at the gas station on the way over, but he told me they didn't have any. I used one of the two condoms he bought instead. It turned out to be a bit more useful.

I had Desmond stuff her mouth with his dick as I slid my hand into the condom. Monica had nipple clips pinching her big chocolate nipples that were almost half as big as her tiny tits. I began to pull on the clips some as she moaned, delighted with the little bit of pain it brought. I reached down between her legs and tried to rub on her clit. She had one of the biggest clits I'd ever seen so far. However, she doesn't seem to be too excited by that. So, I put a finger in her pussy, then two, then three and that's when she began grinding her hips like she wanted to fuck the hell out of my hand.

The position became too awkward as she turned over onto her stomach to continue sucking Desmond's dick. I grabbed a wooden stick and began to spank her hard. With each hit, she grinds her fat clit against the table beneath her and moans. Each time I try to hit harder and harder. She takes a break from sucking to tell me, "That's too hard."

I wanted so badly to do it again and tell her to shut the fuck up. But I know this chick personally, and we're Facebook friends ... blah blah blah. So, I let the shit ride.

I spread her ass, and her asshole opens up just a bit. I spread her ass again, and this time I spit into her open asshole. Then I stick a finger inside her, and I can tell right away, not only does she like it, but there's been plenty of action there. I spit in her ass again to get it good and moist and then began to insert all of my condom covered fingers inside as far as they would go. I could get all five in up to the thumb joint. She's not quite ready to take a fist, but she's getting there. I ram my hand in and out as fast and as hard as I could.

"That's too rough," she complains.

So, I move back down to her pussy. I'm doing the same things there. I motion for Desmond to climb on the table and get in her ass while I'm ramming her pussy. He comes around and does what he's told. After being there a while, he wanted the pussy, so we switched.

I started back ramming her ass. This made Desmond so excited; he pulled out.

"That is some of the sexiest shit I've ever seen," Desmond pants. "All I want to do is watch this shit. Get it, baby."

He spreads her ass as wide as he could allowing my hand to go a little deeper. I did this until I was tired. I had her flip over and told him to finish. I'd done what I came to do actually and was ready to go.

They fucked forever.

"Damn girl, you can really fuck," Desmond says.

Monica's a freak but rarely comes, so they were competing to see who'd tap out first.

I grew sick of that shit.

"Monica," I command. "Hop on top and do your thang."

Shit still takes forever, so she decides to go back to sucking his dick. Before she could put her head down, I whisper, "He likes it in the ass too."

She nods ok and gets down and goes to work. She starts sucking his dick, slobbering up his nuts, and licking under his balls. She then puts one hand on his dick; she's jacking it with that hand. She sucks his balls, and with the other hand, she is fucking the hell out of his ass. His eyes are big, his head is off the table, and he is going crazy. I'm glad he's enjoying it but damn the night was over for me. I was ready to go.

So I grab his dick and start jacking the hell out of it. Do you know that bitch moved my hand like this was *her* dick now?

I let her have it for a minute, but then I had to take it back. Enough was enough. I was tired. I started jacking the shit out of him, and he finally nutted hard and long.

I bent down and kissed him on the cheek and whispered, "I take good care of you?"

"Yes, you sure do," Desmond said out of breath and satisfied.

We packed up into his car and took Monica by a late-night burger joint for a meal. She was just as happy. We dropped her off first, and he drove me back to my car. I didn't want her wet ass in my car.

"Are you satisfied," he asked me.

"Yeah, I guess."

"Well, I know that means I won't hear from you again for at least eight months."

"That's not true," I said unconvinced even as I said it.

"It is," Desmond argued. "It's taking you longer and longer each time."

As I got out of his car, I realized he was right. The thrill of doing this was quickly leaving. Other things were occupying my mind, like God and my baby, Elijah.

A FINAL CONFESSION: GOD FIRST
Elijah

"Who do you love more, me or God?"

So many things happened before the accident that makes me know that it was Elijah's time to leave this fucked up world.

We'd had an amazing year. We took more trips than we ever had. We even took some alone, which was odd since typically I'd been too scared to travel with him on my own, thinking someone would take him from me.

I miss his voice. I can't hear it anymore. I miss his hugs. I even miss his attitude.

However, now I no longer fear the inevitable.

I don't know if I somehow knew my son's life with me would be short or if the way I raised him caused God to want to shorten his life for our sake.

I was fiercely protective of him.

Although Elijah was eleven, I would freak out about him using the men's room. I wanted to know he was ok. I would often get stares as I would kick the men's door open to check on him.

My heart would ache whenever we were apart.

So, Bruce had been right. The 'what ifs' did cross my mind more than they probably should have. I would imagine all sorts of horrible things.

Because of my phobia, throughout my son's life, I kept a journal of the different things we did. At the time, my intention was that it would be a record of his life for him to look back on later.

Turns out, now that he's gone, the journals were written for me. I wish I'd written *and* recorded every single moment of my son's life.

Elijah is in Heaven now, and it hurts, but nothing like earlier this year when he went to Jamestown on a field trip. I guess because I know he is safe now from any harm that I or anyone else could do.

Elijah was an angry baby.

My mom said she'd never seen a baby so full of rage. I remember getting upset with her for pointing out my baby's flaws. I knew it to be true, but it wasn't something I wanted to hear.

I couldn't physically discipline him when he was younger because he would just turn into the hulk (full of rage). I feared he would really hurt himself. People thought I was exaggerating, but you had to see it for yourself.

Elijah didn't really speak until around the age of three, and that's when my baby was diagnosed with a developmental delay. He entered a program and began a new journey. They explained that his anger was most likely due to his developmental issues. He was frustrated at his inability to communicate and express himself.

My baby was everything to me. I very rarely trusted him with anyone and I hated being without him. There were only three people in this world that I was ok with leaving him with and not worrying: his father, his paternal grandmother and one of my aunts. This was because they took watching him very seriously. They kept their eyes on my son the *entire* time he was in their care.

Elijah may have had his issues, but he loved the Lord. He was a praying baby. He loved reading the bible. He prayed for salvation twice and asked to be baptized last year.

My baby is good, and he was the *only* reason I ever got upset with God. I wanted my baby to be off limits to trials and tribulations, but I didn't make the rules, and I wasn't able to change them.

My baby often asked me if I loved him. My answer would vary depending on my mood. "Who do you love more, me or God?" He'd ask.

"Well," I said, "I'm going to say, God, because we're not *supposed* to love anyone or anything more than God. If you do, it's like that person or thing is your God. So, I'm *supposed* to love God more, but to be honest, I feel like I love you more. Let's just say you guys are right there together, but you're just a little lower and only because I'm *supposed* to say that."

Now that God has taken my weakness back home with Him, I can put Him first again.

EPILOGUE
Back To God

I lost my baby in a horrible accident. I struggle between being ok that he is now in the safest place he could ever be in and missing him like crazy.

Everything that happens in my life points me right back to God. That's why even though I *feel* like I'm sick, I *know* God still loves me. He still pulls on my heart. He still wants to help me and probably uses me to reach out to those who are sick to point them back in the right direction.

So really what it comes down to is this struggle between good and evil.

I'm probably not sick after all.

We all have desires. Mine just happens to be to find out the desires of others and tempt them into living them out. I want to see just how far they will go. Playing with the devil probably plays a role in my huge struggle to do right. After all, tempting people to live out their deepest, darkest desires sounds just like something Satan would do, doesn't it?

Sometimes I feel like I'm doing the devil's work and other times I feel like I'm doing the Lord's work. It's enough to make anyone feel like they're crazy, or sick.

Say for example that you desire to eat chocolate. You can never say no to chocolate. Chocolate makes you feel good, and it tastes good. One day you say, "Hey, this thing has a power over me that I don't want it to have."

So, you decide to stop.

You go a whole day without chocolate, but it was hard because all day long, all you could think about was chocolate. You go back and forth in your mind, "I want it. I don't. I do. I don't." Finally, you ask, "What's wrong with me? Nothing's wrong with eating chocolate. Why deny myself?"

So, you eat some. Alas, you feel defeated and guilty because chocolate won again.

I believe that what makes something wrong is your conviction. It's all about relationships. It's not a problem unless *you* feel it's a problem. If it's a problem for *you*, then no matter what anyone else thinks, it's a problem indeed.

There's internal conflict, and because of this internal conflict, a person feels crazy or sick.

Elijah once said that if I were a superhero, my name would be Struggle Girl. He saw me struggle through life.

I'm probably one of the most irresponsible adults ever, but I loved my son fiercely.

Every year while he was in elementary school, I urged them to pass him. They said he'd never be an A student, but I knew that if he could just get to middle school things would pan out. He made it to middle school, and just as I suspected, he was able to make A's and B's.

At the time of his passing, he had a 100 in math, a few more A's and B's and one F that we were working on. For the first time in a while, I was hard on him about that F. It wasn't the grade, but the fact that he was having behavioral issues in this particular class. He was also not doing his work in the class, earning 0's on tests.

I'd always told him to try his best, and I'll fix the rest, but he wasn't even trying.

Had I known what was to come, I wouldn't have even cared about that F.

Earlier this year, I ran across a bag that had a few things in it for my son from a company we'd visited together to set up his finances. In that bag, I found an insurance policy we'd gotten for him that day.

I'd given Elijah all the things from the bag that were his and then I had no idea where I'd put the policy. I'd forgotten I'd even purchased one for him until I unexpectedly came upon it again.

I can only think that it was God preparing me for when the time came that I'd have to use that policy and make the ultimate sacrifice of giving my son back to God.

Book Club Discussion

Can you truly live a double life? What are the downfalls of doing so?

Morgan talked about glitches, tethers, and transference. Can you relate to these terms? How so?

Does love hurt? Should it? Why or why not?

What are your thoughts concerning 'the voices' that Morgan hears?

Have you ever been angry with God? Why?

Do intentions matter? Do they matter more than actions? Why or why not?

Do you consider Morgan to be an abusive person? Sick? Selfish?

If you're sick, would you know that you're sick?

Can you relate to any parts of this story?

A Word from The Author

Although this story ended, I have not come to a resolution. I realize the best I can hope for is that at some point I'll be a better person. And if not, at least I can inspire someone else to journey towards their better life.

I grabbed one of my grandma's bibles, and although I wasn't turning the pages yet, it flipped right to the section about Elijah. It's a study bible, so it gives commentary on the section that is referenced. One of the parts says, "Elijah came to confront, not comfort."

Though my baby gave me great comfort, I believe his main purpose was to confront me. I find it eerie that he left just as I was allowing myself to come to certain realities.

That's just how God works in my life – everything is **BIG** and almost *unbelievable.*

Maybe He knows that in my case, **BIG** and *unbelievable* is what is needed to get and keep my attention.

www.ingramcontent.com/pod-product-compliance
Lightning Source LLC
Chambersburg PA
CBHW070508030726
47503CB00004B/1205